"You're going _____
Age," Bruce began, hesitantly.

"No, I won't .Trust me," Gayle coaxed him, her curiosity aroused.

"I've never kissed a girl" Bruce blurted out. "I'm probably the only guy at Glenwood High who hasn't. When I go out with Cheryl tomorrow night, I know she'll expect me to. But I'm worried that I'll do it wrong and blow everything."

There was a stunned silence. Gayle tried to think of how to reply. But standing so close to Bruce made her feel slightly light-headed. He looked so handsome, and when she looked into his hazel eyes, the words stuck in her throat. Suddenly she was afraid.

"I know it sounds dumb," Bruce said, "but it's the only thing none of you taught me."

Don't ask me to do it, Bruce, Gayle thought desperately. *Don't torture me this way. If you only knew how much I care—*

"Please say you'll help me," Bruce continued, moving toward her, "Please kiss me, Gayle."

Meet Glenwood High's fabulous four, the

SENIORS

Kit, Elaine, Alex, and Lori are very best friends.
Every girl's ideal, every boy's dream. These popular seniors
share all their hopes, fears, and deepest secrets.

On the brink of graduation and adulthood, they're discovering
themselves, planning for the future . . . and falling in love. Don't
miss them!

Ask your bookseller for titles you have missed:

1. TOO MUCH, TOO SOON
2. SMART ENOUGH TO KNOW
3. WINNER ALL THE WAY
4. AFRAID TO LOVE
5. BEFORE IT'S TOO LATE
6. TOO HOT TO HANDLE
7. HANDS OFF HE'S MINE
8. FORBIDDEN KISSES
9. A TOUCH OF GINGER

Coming soon:

11. BAD GIRL
12. DON'T SAY GOODBYE

PRESENTING SUPERHUNK
by Eileen Goudge

BANTAM BOOKS
TORONTO • NEW YORK • LONDON • SYDNEY • AUCKLAND

PRESENTING SUPERHUNK
A Bantam Book / June 1987

ISBN 0-553-17372 3

Bantam Books are published by Bantam Books, Inc.
Its trademark, consisting of the words "Bantam
Books" and the portrayal of a rooster, is Registered in
U.S. Patent and Trademark Office
and in other countries.
Marca Registrada, Bantam Books, Inc.,
666 Fifth Avenue,
New York, New York 10103

Reproduced, printed and bound in Great Britain by
Hazell Watson & Viney Limited,
Member of the BPCC Group,
Aylesbury, Bucks

Chapter One

Kit McCoy was calling it Operation Super-hunk, but Gayle Rodgers thought it sounded more like Mission Impossible.

Or at least Mission Improbable. It wasn't that she thought Bruce Fletcher was beyond redemption. Quite the contrary. She thought the brown-haired, hazel-eyed boy was on the cute side, even though his slicked back, side-parted hair looked as if it'd been combed by an overzealous mother and he had this annoying habit of clipping his pens in the pockets of his shirts. It was just that Kit wasn't talking about changing one thing about Bruce—she wanted to change *everything*.

More than any of the other girls sitting in Kit's cramped bedroom Gayle knew how hard it was to undergo a transformation. She had just completed the difficult task of losing sixty pounds, and it had taken every ounce of willpower and strength she could muster. "Are you sure Bruce really wants to do this?" Gayle asked Kit, her voice betraying her hesitancy in speaking up.

Kit looked at Gayle from her perch on her dresser. "Of course he does," she said, her blue eyes sparkling from beneath her blond curls. "At least he did after I got through convincing him what a good idea it would be. Just think, after we finish making him over, Bruce Fletcher is going to be the primo boy at Glenwood High."

"Jeez, you make him sound like a basket case," Alex Enomoto pointed out from the corner of Kit's bed—unmade as usual. "But you can count me in, I've always been attracted to lost causes."

"No, I don't mean that at all," Kit said, defending herself. Once again she told her friends about her plan to teach the newly transplanted Chicago boy how to dress, talk, and act like a true Californian. "I wouldn't be bothering if I thought Bruce was a total nerd. There's just something about him that tells me—I don't know—that somewhere underneath those blue Oxford shirts and wing-tip shoes lies a guy with great potential."

Lori Woodhouse raised one of her blond eyebrows, an impish smile crossing her exquisitely sculpted face. "What's the matter, Kit. Getting tired of Justin?"

Kit opened her eyes wide in mock horror. "Moi?" she cried, shaking her blond curls violently. "Never. I just hate to see such potential wasted. Besides, Bruce only has eyes for another girl."

"I should have known," Elaine Gregory said, narrowing her nutmeg-colored eyes and tossing her shoulder-length brown hair. "Kit McCoy—hopeless romantic and matchmaker to all at Glenwood High. Who does he have eyes for?"

Kit paused dramatically. "Cheryl Abrahamson," she announced. The news brought a collective groan from the group, which Kit dissipated by waving her hands for quiet. "Look, she's not my idea of the ideal girl, either, but that's not the point. I've gotten to know Bruce a little in the past few weeks. Glenwood's another world compared to Chicago. He's feeling a little out of place, unsure of himself. It's not easy being a new person at school, especially when you transfer in the middle of senior year. Wouldn't you agree, Gayle?"

Gayle looked around the room at her new friends. Kit had hit home in a big way. Not too long ago she'd been the new one, and her loneliness and fear of rejection were still fresh in her memory. Brushing a curl out of her wide brown eyes, she replied, "You're right, Kit. He'll appreciate getting all the attention."

But inside, Gayle wasn't so sure. It was one thing when people flocked to your side to let

3

you know how much they admired you, quite another when the only thing on their mind was telling you what lousy shape you were in.

Gayle kept these thoughts to herself. She was still too new to the group to threaten the tentative friendship by questioning Kit's plan. She knew Kit felt she was doing the right thing. In the short time they'd been friends it'd been easy to see that Kit didn't have a malicious bone in her body. Besides, everyone else seemed to think it sounded like a great idea.

"Just think, this is kind of like being Dr. Frankenstein," cried Alex, the athlete of the group, her brown eyes twinkling mischievously as she rubbed her hands together, feigning a fiendish glee. "Only instead of creating a monster, we'll be creating a sex symbol."

"Did someone mention sex?" Stephanie, Alex's new foster sister, looked up from the copy of *Cosmo* Kit had flung carelessly on the floor next to her bed. "Now, this is getting interesting...."

"Well, if we're here to teach him how to do *It* then I'm leaving," Elaine said, pretending to rise from Kit's desk chair. "That's not my specialty."

"You're telling us!" Alex countered with a wink. "But then, we could always give you some lessons, too."

Gayle felt both flustered and amused by the conversation. She loved to listen to her friends' easy bantering, yet she had a hard time bringing herself to join in and marveled at how Elaine simply shrugged off Alex's retort. But then Gayle had heard they'd been friends practically since birth. Sex lessons. She shivered, fascinated by the thought. She could barely say the word, let alone imagine what it would be like to actually go to bed with a boy.

Not too long ago, though, no boy would have even considered dating her, Gayle reflected. When she came to Glenwood from San Francisco she was quite overweight, more like a carrot-topped jelly bean than the slender green bean she'd always longed to be. And she might have been doomed to buying her clothes at Lane Bryant forever if she hadn't met Lori. The slender blonde was sensitive enough to give Gayle the courage and inspiration to discover the inner strength in herself that enabled her to shed those unwanted pounds.

She stared down at her yellow cotton blouse, belted at the waist, and her electric green pants. The colors went well with her long, red hair, and now that she was able to fit into stylish clothes like these, she was starting to draw attention from boys at school. Nothing serious, but even a smile was a new experience for her to deal with. If this new attention kept up, Gayle reflected, not only could she use sex lessons; she'd need an entire education on the male of the species.

Maybe Kit's idea wasn't so farfetched after all, she realized. Maybe Bruce really wanted to change the way he was—just as she had—and saw Kit's plan as a way to do so. Anyway, she reasoned, he probably had nothing to lose. She knew all too well what it was like to feel left out.

"Gayle? Gayle?" Kit called as she waved her hands in front of Gayle. "Are you with us or not?"

Gayle shook herself out of her thoughts. "You bet, Kit. I—I was just thinking about something."

"I'm glad to see someone around here's thinking," quipped Kit. "Anyway, are you going to help us fix up Bruce?"

Gayle nodded, then couldn't resist adding, "If it works, can we take the new Bruce to science class with our before-and-after pictures and get credit for the experiment?" Someone threw a sock at her, and Gayle quickly said, "When do we begin?"

"I had a feeling you were going to volunteer me for this," remarked Lori. Gayle couldn't help picking up the air of reluctance in Lori's voice. Was she having doubts about this plan, too? Lori was Gayle's closest friend in the group and someone nobody would have ever believed had a weight problem. With her naturally sparkling good looks, she was considered one of the prettiest girls in school. Not only did she have a flair for fashion, she'd even done some modeling around town and hoped to become a professional model. "I'll take him to the mall this weekend."

"Fine. Once he's dressed right, I'll teach him to dance," Kit continued. Everyone nodded their approval. Kit would be perfect at that, Gayle noted. Bound for Julliard in the fall, Kit could dance circles around anyone at Glenwood. If Bruce could learn to keep up with her, he'd be set for life.

"I'll work with Kit and give Bruce some tips on sophistication," volunteered Ginger. Kit's tall, slender cousin from New York was spending her final months of high school in Glenwood while her mother was in Europe.

"Don't forget about flirting!" Elaine broke in. "Even if he knows how to dance, he's still going to need to know what to say to his date afterward."

"Good thinking, Elaine," said Kit. "I'll take care of that. Now, Alex, I need you to teach Bruce a sport." Kit put her index finger to her mouth, as she thought. "Cheryl loves to play tennis, so I think that would be a good place to start."

"Maybe I'll teach him how to surf, too," added Alex.

"Hey, let's do one sport at a time," Elaine said. "The guy's going to have enough to learn as it is."

"Wait a second," jumped in Stephanie, a trace of her usual scowl in her voice. "What good is it to know how to flirt, dance, and play tennis if you don't have that certain class of cool that cuts through all the bull and really grabs at your heart?"

Everyone agreed, although Gayle wondered how something like that could be taught. "That'll be your assignment, Stephanie," Kit said.

"Deal," Stephanie shot back. She paused. "Hey, I'm liking this more and more as we speak."

"I'll coordinate all of this," Elaine said. "Bruce is going to need some strategy on how to use all of these newfound skills. I'll teach him when to flirt and when not to, where to start up conversations and when to play hard to get. I'll be his coach, his Cyrano de Bergerac."

"Great. Just don't let your nose get too big," joked Alex, wrinkling her own nose, which she often complained was too small.

"If this works, we just might be creating the sexiest guy at the whole school," Kit remarked thoughtfully.

"Yeah, maybe we should bottle our plan and sell it. We'd make a fortune," added Alex.

"You know, that's not a bad idea . . . to go into the consulting business, I mean," suggested Stephanie, genuinely intrigued. "There are a lot of nerds out there . . ."

"Bruce isn't a nerd," interrupted Kit.

"I know, I don't mean Bruce," continued Stephanie. "I mean boys in general. Sometimes boys are really . . . well, they are really . . ."

"Idiots!" finished Kit. "I know what you mean."

Gayle hadn't said a word. She'd never had a boyfriend to be exasperated with. She let her thoughts drift to Bruce, wondering what he would think if he could hear them now. He just wanted to feel comfortable at Glenwood, make some new friends, and maybe get Cheryl to notice him. Who could blame him for that? Gayle thought back to the time she'd talked to him.

The image had yet to fade. The picnic, the park, the other kids laughing, and, of course, the egg, were as crystal clear in Gayle's mind as if it had happened yesterday—instead of nearly a month ago...

Somehow she and Bruce had been put together as partners for the egg toss at the class picnic. Looking back, Gayle realized he was probably the only one there who hadn't known what a fatso she had been. She, in turn, was probably the only one who hadn't been put off by the decidedly unstylish blue shirt and navy dress pants he'd worn to school nearly every day like a uniform. After years of having longed for boys to look beyond her body to the nice person inside, she knew better than to judge someone only on surface appearance. She smiled at him, but all she was greeted with was a shy grin.

Gayle had worn her favorite outfit to the picnic, a Laura Ashley pioneer dress that showed off her newly slender figure. She'd have died if she'd gotten a raw egg all over it, so she was extra careful with each toss of the egg. Bruce had been careful, too, not like most of the guys who hadn't cared if they broke their eggs or not.

To her great surprise, moving farther and farther apart with each toss, they had been one of the last surviving couples. This had made Gayle even more nervous. Suddenly, everyone was *looking* at her.

She had been so unnerved that her next toss had been a bad one. It was way too high and not far enough. Bruce had run forward to try to get under it. He'd reached up over his head as he ran, trying to make a valiant catch, but the egg had gone right through both outstretched hands. It had been a bull's eye...egg all over his face! Everyone had roared with laughter. Gayle's cheeks had turned as red as her hair. At first, it didn't look as if Bruce were too happy, but finally he'd managed a laugh and Gayle had sighed with relief.

Turning Bruce into a superhunk was going to be a challenge, she realized. But Kit had managed to cover all the bases. Everyone there was able to contribute her best talent to the cause. Everyone but...

"Um, what about me?" Gayle asked her friends as she racked her brain for any helpful hints she could offer.

"There are lots of things you could help him with," Lori said.

"Like what? He doesn't need help losing weight," groaned Gayle, actually beginning to get worried.

There was a short, awkward pause as everyone tried to think of something for Gayle to do. Finally Lori came to the rescue.

"He doesn't know how to drive. You could teach him!"

"Yeah, that's the most important thing of all. If he can't drive he'll never be able to go out on dates," added Kit.

Lori continued. "You're the only one who can do it. Besides Alex, you're the only one of us who's got her own car."

"And asking Bruce to drive the Green Demon would be sadistic," joked Elaine. Alex had a beat up old Dodge Dart that was legendary both in its tendency to break down and Alex's ability to repair it.

"You mean he doesn't know how to drive?" asked Stephanie. "Where's he been — on the moon?"

"No, Chicago," explained Kit. "It's a big city, and he didn't have to know. He always took the bus or a taxi or walked. But he's got his learner's permit — he told me."

"No wonder he's having trouble adjusting to California," Stephanie commented.

"All right, enough picking on Bruce. It's settled. Gayle will teach him how to drive," said Elaine. "Do you think you could get started soon — like tomorrow?"

"Sure," Gayle said, gulping as the realization of what was about to happen sank in. She could barely say "good morning" to a boy without the words getting stuck in her throat. How in the world would she teach a boy to drive?

Chapter Two

"A clutch?"

"It's a stick shift."

"Oh, no, talk about jumping in over your head with both feet," moaned Bruce as he surveyed the inside of Gayle's VW bug.

"It's really not that difficult," Gayle assured her nervous pupil, feeling a sense of panic rise up inside her. This wasn't going to be easy, and she had half a mind to leave Bruce right there on the street outside Glenwood High and let him take the school bus home.

"Well, at least I use my left foot for the clutch. Most people think I've got two left feet anyway, so maybe that'll help," Bruce kidded. Nervously he ran his hand through his brown hair, while his hazel eyes darted over the car's dashboard trying to get acquainted with everything.

Gayle was concerned. She wished Kit and Alex had started on their confidence-building lessons first. Bruce didn't appear sure of himself at all. She'd better figure out a way to help him relax, so he wouldn't feel pressured and have a hard time learning.

"Don't worry, you'll do fine," she said, trying to convince herself at the same time. "But don't be disappointed if I haven't got you qualified for the Indy 500 by the end of the day."

"That's tomorrow's lesson, right?" Bruce countered, looking over at his teacher. His warm, direct smile and sense of humor touched her, and all at once, Gayle felt hopeful.

"Have you read the driving manual?" she asked.

"Yeah. I'm sure I could pass the written test with my eyes closed. But this is the first time I've been behind the wheel," he said.

"You'll do fine," she repeated.

She strapped on her seat belt over her new green blouse and turned to him. "We'll take this nice and easy. First start the car."

"Right." He looked at her blankly.

"With the key. You turn it," she said, pointing, and thinking that he was joking until she recognized the look of terror in Bruce's eyes. She winced again. The afternoon was going to be worse than she'd thought.

"Oh, yeah, of course. Gee, you must think

I'm dumb." Bruce laughed nervously.

"Oh, no. Don't worry, Bruce," she said, trying to think of something to calm him down. "You should've seen me when I was first learning. I was a real wreck. I couldn't tell the gas from the brake. But I learned—and you will, too."

"Okay. Here we go." Bruce turned the key to start the car, and immediately it lurched forward, almost hitting the parked car in front of them. "Mistake number one," he said with a sheepish smile.

"Let's not count them," Gayle suggested, smiling.

"Good, I think I'm going to like you as a teacher," Bruce said, his eyes sparkling with genuine appreciation at her patience.

Gayle noticed the sparkle, and her smile gained a little warmth as she responded, "It was my fault. I forgot to tell you to take it out of gear before you start it. Neutral's here. Can you feel it?" she asked, as she jiggled the gear shift back and forth in the middle. As their hands brushed, Gayle felt a tingle rise up her arm. Even though it was only an accidental touch, she felt pleasantly flustered.

"Yeah, I got it," he assured her. He turned the key and it started right up.

"Okay, now what?" he asked.

"Put it in reverse and we'll back out of here," Gayle told him. If she'd been better at flirting—like Kit—she would have guided his hand through the shifting operation, just for the thrill of touching him again. But she kept her hands buried in her lap.

"Reverse!" he blurted out, mock panic sweeping across his face. "Nobody told me about reverse!"

"Well, we can't go forward any farther," she responded pointing to the car in front.

"We could just sit and wait until the owner came along and moved it," he suggested.

"But it's hard to learn to drive just sitting here," Gayle answered, trying to keep a straight face.

"Okay, so how do I find reverse?"

"You push down, and shift it to the left."

"Could you show me?"

The request startled her. But she did as he asked, putting her hand over his warm one and showing him the difficult procedure typical of all Volkswagens. She felt a little giddy, being so close to Bruce and all, but she forced herself to concentrate on the lesson. "Now, slowly let out the clutch and rev up the engine a little," Gayle instructed as she looked back behind the car. "You've got plenty of room."

Bruce pressed down on the gas pedal slightly and turned to look back where he was going. They sat there for a moment as he slowly let out the clutch—so slowly that nothing happened. Finally, in frustration, he quickly popped it out. The car lurched backward in a fitful leap, and the engine died. They had moved four feet.

"Not bad. Try again," Gayle said encouragingly.

This time Bruce managed to move it back about ten feet before he killed the engine. He was looking a bit frustrated.

"Don't worry. We've got enough room now in front so you can put it in first. That's a lot easier than reverse — at least for *most* people," she added, challengingly.

"Right, but I'm warning you. I've got some A.J. Foyt in my blood." With that, Bruce let out the clutch and lurched forward down the street. Once he got going he did fairly well. Until it came time to shift, that is.

"Go ahead and shift into second, but remember to put in the clutch," Gayle told him.

"Okay, watch this," he announced confidently.

He pushed in the clutch but forgot to take his foot off the accelerator. The engine revved up too fast, but Bruce didn't notice it; he was too busy making a smooth shift to second and quickly letting out the clutch. The engine was going so fast as a result that when the clutch engaged, the VW jumped forward, laying the first patch of rubber in its long life. The sudden speed scared Bruce so much that he panicked and put both feet on the brake, bringing the car to an immediate halt. Gayle gripped the front of the dashboard, her knuckles white.

"I'm sorry! I didn't mean to do that!" he said, looking at her with genuine concern. "I feel like such a dummy."

Bruce's despair summoned up a rush of sympathy in Gayle. She relaxed her grip and tried to offer Bruce an encouraging smile. "That's okay, nobody's hurt. Go ahead, let's try again."

He started up the car, and eventually they arrived safely at an empty parking lot surrounded by small elm trees at the Little League baseball park.

"Thank goodness, we're here. I only killed it four times," announced Bruce, sounding very relieved not to have hit anything.

"Remember, I said we wouldn't count the mistakes," Gayle said.

"If only my teachers felt the same way!" Bruce said, jokingly. "Seriously, I don't know how you can be so patient, Gayle. I'm sure glad to be learning with you and not with one of my parents. I don't think they'd stay the course."

"Good thinking. I remember how my father tore his hair out with me. I think there ought to be a rule: thou shalt not teach thy child how to drive."

"Just think, now I'll be able to chauffeur everyone around town."

"All the girls?" Gayle joked.

"As many as I can fit in the car," Bruce said, grinning. "No, I'm not what you'd call a ladies' man, Gayle. I was talking about my family."

"Do you have any brothers or sisters?"

"Four brothers—all younger. I'm adopted,

18

actually, although my brothers aren't. My parents call us their basketball team. What about you, Gayle?"

Gayle was surprised that Bruce could admit so confidently that he was adopted. *He must feel really secure about his parents' love and his role in the family to be able to do that,* she thought, wistfully.

"A brother and a sister. But they're both a lot older than I am, so it's almost like I'm an only child." Gayle tried to hide the pain she felt whenever the subject of her family came up. "It must be nice to have such a large family."

He nodded. "It's helped make the move here easier for me. I sort of miss my old friends."

"I know what you mean. I moved here from San Francisco at the beginning of the year. It was hard for me to get used to Glenwood. I used to go to an all-girls school, and it was a shock going co-ed."

"Really? I went to an all boys' Catholic school in Chicago. I hated it. I mean, it was a good school and all, but I had to wear this awful uniform—with a tie and everything."

"So did I! The same blue plaid skirt and white blouse every day." Gayle laughed, surprised that they had these things in common. "So Glenwood really is a change for you." No wonder he didn't know how to dress, she thought, casting a wary look at his wide-cut, white short-sleeved shirt and his ill-fitting Levis.

"Yeah, but I think I like it out here," Bruce continued. "Things are more relaxed, or at least they seem that way. But I do miss one of my classes—astronomy. We had the best teacher....".

"You like astronomy?" asked Gayle, excited. "I do, too. I know all the constellations, and I love to read about it. I go to the Stanford Observatory every once in a while. It's fun."

"I have a telescope of my own. I built it myself!" Bruce proudly told her.

"You did? That sounds pretty difficult," Gayle said, impressed.

She wanted to tell Bruce about her own hobby of photography, but she hesitated. No one in Glenwood knew about it, not even Lori. It was something very special to her, something she took very seriously, and she was afraid to open herself to criticism. Her interest had begun several years ago, when her uncle had given her an old, beat-up Nikon and a couple of lenses. She'd taken up photography pretty seriously since then and now worked mostly in black-and-white. She especially loved to do the studies of different subjects, varying the time of day, the lighting, the exposure, or whatever else she could think of to come up with unusual and creative shots.

"Actually, it wasn't all that hard to build it. You buy a kit and follow directions. But anyhow, you'll have to come over and see it!" he said, obviously excited at finding someone who shared his interest.

"That sounds great. I'd love to," Gayle responded. She hesitated only for a moment before plunging forward, encouraged by Bruce's enthusiasm. "I built something, too."

"A telescope?" he asked.

"No, a camera."

"That's incredible!" he exclaimed. There was a look of genuine interest on his increasingly handsome face.

"It really was very easy. You see, photography's sort of my hobby. I shoot a lot of black-and-white, and I can work in a dark room and stuff. One of my teachers showed us how to make a camera out of a shoebox."

"A shoebox! You're kidding. How does it work?"

"You just make a pin hole at one end and a place for the film plate at the other end." Gayle began to explain, relieved to see how much easier it was to converse with Bruce than she'd ever have believed. To her amazement, he seemed to enjoy talking to her, too.

In the back of her mind a jealous little thought began to form. She wished that Bruce hadn't revealed to Kit that he had a crush on Cheryl. It was turning out that Bruce was far more interesting than he had at first appeared. Besides, Gayle wasn't so sure about Cheryl for Bruce. She had a reputation for being a gossip; and as Gayle knew all too well from her PE class, Cheryl was kind of stuck on herself. But then Gayle couldn't really blame Bruce; Cheryl was definitely very cute and—as head cheerleader—very popular. A lot of boys liked her, a lot more than liked Gayle. But then that wasn't too hard, she thought: the number of boys who liked her was a big, fat zero.

"Wait, a minute, we're not moving," she joked, shaking out of her head the image of Bruce and Cheryl arm in arm. "You're supposed to be learning how to drive, not sitting here chatting."

They spent the next half hour driving around in circles in the parking lot as Bruce practiced shifting, stopping, starting, and turning around. At first he was clumsy, having a hard time synchronizing his feet and hands as he shifted, but he learned quickly. By the end of the lesson Gayle was willing to let him drive back to his house.

Bruce was very determined to redeem himself.

"I'm not going to kill it once, you just watch," he assured her as he pulled into one of the narrow roads near his hillside house.

"Bruce, I feel so confident about your ability, I'm not even going to watch," Gayle said, daringly. Intoxicated by the success of their afternoon, she shut her eyes and leaned back dramatically in her seat. As she thought about the progress they had made that day, Bruce carried on a running commentary, describing what he was doing as he did it.

"Now I signal with the blinker to turn left, waiting for the car ahead to come past me, and now I am turning left. Easy!" He seemed very pleased with it all, but suddenly they heard a car horn beeping incessantly at them.

"What's wrong with that guy? Hey! That car's coming straight at me!" Bruce exclaimed in panic.

Gayle's eyes flew open as she snapped out of her daydreaming. Looking around, she realized immediately what had gone wrong. "It's a one-way street! We're going the wrong way!" she screeched, terrified they might crash. "Pull over, fast!"

Bruce turned the wheel so quickly that he ran the car up on the curb, nearly colliding with a nearby fire hydrant. Confidence rushed out of him like the air from a balloon. Despite her own sense of panic, Gayle couldn't help being reminded of the day he caught the egg with his face.

"Just when I thought I was doing so well," he moaned.

"Don't worry about it. It's not that big of a deal," she said, trying to comfort him. She had been genuinely frightened herself, but she didn't want Bruce to get depressed.

"It's actually a good thing," she continued. "I had been planning to discuss parallel parking on the next lesson, but now that you bring it up let me point out that two wheels on the curb is going a little bit overboard," she deadpanned.

Bruce turned to look at her in disbelief, still feeling pretty bad about his goof. But when he noticed the sparkle in her eye he quickly replied, "I didn't want you to have to walk very far to the curb." They both burst out laughing.

"Actually, Bruce, you did very well for the first day. You shouldn't be discouraged," Gayle told him seriously.

"Well, naturally. I've got a pretty good teacher, after all," he said.

"You just need a few more lessons," she encouraged him, pleased by the compliment.

"You mean Operation Superhunk," Bruce said. Gayle started to say that wasn't what she meant, but Bruce continued. "Yes, it looks as if my life is suddenly to be filled with strange and mysterious happenings. But unlike Eliza Doolittle, I think I know what I'm in for. I was a bit doubtful about Kit's idea at first. I mean, a hunk? Me?"

"You do?" asked Gayle.

"Well, I know *whom* I'll be surrounded by during the metamorphosis, and that's something I can't complain about," Bruce said, looking directly at Gayle.

There was a strange flutter in her heart, and all at once, Gayle felt at a loss for words. He meant all of them, of course—spending time with so many different girls.

"Good," she declared. "Now, I think I had better get us out of this."

Gayle took over and drove Bruce home. They agreed to meet for lessons every other day until they felt he was ready for his driver's test.

"See you the day after tomorrow," she said, as she pulled up in front of his house.

"Thanks a lot for everything, Gayle, you were great," her student told her. Then, after shaking her hand, Bruce let himself out of the car.

She watched as Bruce happily bounded up his driveway, hopped over two bicycles left in his path and, with a final wave from the porch, disappeared into the house. For a long moment, Gayle didn't move. Her heart beat loudly and her cheeks flushed with warmth. She was surprised at how affected she had been by the touch of his hand. She didn't know quite how to explain this rush of excitement, but one thing was for sure. She couldn't wait for the next lesson.

Chapter Three

During their next lesson Gayle was amazed to hear what Bruce's schedule was like for the rest of the week. Almost every afternoon or evening was taken up with one of the girls instructing him in the fine art of sex appeal—or "superhunkdom" as Stephanie put it. But Bruce didn't complain about his lack of free time. Quite the contrary. No wonder he never acted embarrassed by their plan to "make him over," Gayle realized. He was too busy planning to enjoy all that attention.

Their third driving lesson was scheduled to follow a tennis session with Alex. Gayle decided to drop by the Glenwood High courts early to watch from the sidelines. She was curious to see how one of the other girls fared with Bruce.

"Keep your wrists straight!" yelled Alex, as Gayle walked up. "And don't be afraid to really hit it."

"Oh, you mean the object is to get the ball over the net?" Bruce laughed. "I keep thinking of squash and looking for a wall."

Bruce stroked a ball to Alex with a surprising amount of topspin on it, but Alex, a graceful blur of tennis whites, returned it effortlessly and accurately. The ball bounced in an easy position for Bruce to return it. To his apparent amazement, he did.

"Good shot," Alex called out breathlessly as she gave chase.

Her backhand stroke was picture perfect, but her shot forced Bruce to shift too radically and get too far under the ball. It shot up into the air like a frightened quail and landed in a tree behind the tennis courts.

Alex watched the flight of the ball with a decided air of resignation. "Well, you definitely got it over the net that time. When you bend your wrist like that it can get a little tricky."

"Sorry," groaned Bruce, glancing over at Gayle sheepishly.

"I'll get it!" offered Gayle.

"That's okay, let's call it a day," Alex said, as she took off her baby blue headband and shook out her short black hair.

"Okay," Bruce said, not looking the least bit disappointed.

"Remember, this Saturday we go surfing,"

Alex reminded him, as she put the rackets back in their covers. All three headed for the tree to collect the ball.

"I'd better bring a life jacket," he said as they walked.

"Can't you swim?" Alex asked with alarm.

"Sure. But you don't get ten-foot waves in Lake Michigan," he responded, with some genuine concern.

"Don't worry, you'll love it. Surfing is absolutely the most fun. You'll probably end up a surfing bum. Besides, we'll be lucky if there are five-foot swells," she said.

"Swell by me," he joked, straightfaced. Then he jumped up and started to climb the tree to get the ball.

Alex looked at him, rolled her eyes, and groaned, "You're a real sport, Bruce, you really are."

In Gayle's opinion, Alex was so good at everything she attempted that she could come across as pretty intimidating sometimes—especially to a novice like Bruce. Gayle herself was often in awe of Alex's grace and commitment to excellence. Obviously, it wasn't all smooth sailing for Bruce.

"See you Saturday, Alex," he called out, tossing her the ball.

Gayle and Bruce headed for her car, and Alex waved good-bye. "I see Lori took you shopping. I like those shorts," Gayle offered, admiring the way they showed off Bruce's trim—yet still untanned—legs. She wondered if he would notice the new yellow Esprit sweater she had on.

"Thanks. Lori's so kindhearted, she has a hard time telling me my taste in clothes stinks," Bruce said as they headed for her car and another driving lesson.

"Nobody has the fashion sense that Lori has. She's got a natural eye," Gayle told him.

"It was funny yesterday. We were at some store at the mall and she was having me try on clothes, holding up shirts and pants and telling me how good I'd look in them. I was enjoying it, but then this older saleswoman came over. She told Lori that she really knew how to dress her brother."

"Really!"

"Yeah, we both started to laugh, and the lady looked kind of embarrassed. Then Lori told her that I wasn't her brother, but her boyfriend!" Bruce said, his amazement still showing.

"She did?" exclaimed Gayle. The news bothered her, though she couldn't figure out why.

"I was so shocked I must have turned three shades of red. Lori couldn't stop laughing. I'm sure the saleswoman thought we were crazy," he said.

"Sometimes Lori can surprise you. You never know with her. She's always so nice and concerned and sensitive. Then all of a sudden she can say something unexpected and really funny. I think that's part of why I like her so much," Gayle explained.

"You know, it's kind of strange," Bruce went on. "But I've noticed that since you girls began helping me, other kids are wondering how I rate to be hanging around with all these great-looking girls. I even think Cheryl's noticed me."

"Have you talked to her?" Gayle asked.

"Well, I said hello to her in the hallway, and she looked at me really strangely. Then I blew it, though, I didn't know what to say. I think I need some more pointers from Elaine," he responded, his former enthusiasm slipping.

Part of Gayle wanted to hear how Cheryl was reacting to Bruce's transformation and part of her didn't. In fact, she didn't know if she could handle it if he told her how much he liked Cheryl. But before either of them could say anything more, they arrived at the car, and the conversation shifted to their driving lesson.

"I've got it!" Lori shouted later that evening. Her friend's cry jolted Gayle from *Crime and Punishment*, a book she was reading for her literature class. "What is it?" Gayle asked, looking toward her rolltop desk, where Lori was bent over a pile of paper. "Did you discover gold up there or something?"

Lori turned to Gayle with a big smile on her face. "Even better," she said. "I finally figured out the answer to this calculus problem. It was driving me crazy. Sorry if I scared you."

31

"Not to worry," Gayle said, rubbing her eyes. Rising to a sitting position on her bed, she tossed aside the book. "I've had about as many Russians as I can take for the time being. Feel like taking a break?"

Lori threw down her pencil. "After cracking that problem I feel like celebrating."

"Good. Let's go downstairs and raid the refrigerator."

A few minutes later the two girls were seated at the Rodgers' butcher block kitchen table, their "feast" in front of them. With relish, they dug their spoons into matching containers of low-fat strawberry yogurt.

Gayle remembered when things were different. "Not too long ago, I would have been sitting here with a giant bowlful of ice cream and hot fudge sauce," she added.

"I would have added whipped cream and almonds," Lori put in.

"And don't forget the cherry on top," Gayle concluded. She dropped her spoon into the half-eaten cup. "Wow, six months ago if you told me I'd be stuffed after eating a couple of spoonfuls of yogurt, I'd have thought you were nuts."

"It just goes to show what you can do when you put your mind to it," Lori said, eyeing her friend. "Hey, those shorts look a little loose on you."

Gayle looked down at her cutoffs. "They do, don't they? According to my scale I lost two pounds last week."

"Bravo, amigo," Lori cried happily.

"I'm glad you could come over and study with me tonight. It helps to have someone around."

"How long are your parents going to be away, this time?" Lori asked.

"They're in L.A. till Friday. Then they're going to spend the weekend at our condo in Rancho Mirage. Not that it really matters," she added quickly.

Gayle's parents had gone to Los Angeles for a restaurant convention. But the two of them were out of the house so often that she felt as if she were living there alone most of the time. Her father, a retired businessman, usually spent much of the day playing golf. Her mother was devoted to her gourmet restaurant and catering service in San Francisco.

Gayle was, as her mother tactfully put it, a "change of life" baby, born when her brother and sister were in college and her parents were well into their forties. No matter how many times they told her how much they loved her, however, Gayle couldn't help thinking it was their way of trying to cover up the truth—that she'd been a mistake. She hated the way her father always winced whenever a passerby on the street referred to him as her grandfather. When her mother had presented her with her own credit card to The Emporium for her fourteenth birthday, she'd told Gayle how wonderful it would be for her to shop without a mother looking over her

33

shoulder. Gayle never told anyone how she had cried herself to sleep that night, convinced her mother had given her the card only to get Gayle out of her way and to make things easier for herself.

Gayle had hoped things would have changed after she lost all that weight, but to her dismay they hadn't. Her mother had remarked how pleased she was and told Gayle she'd treat her to a new wardrobe—a promise that was yet to be fulfilled. But her father, Gayle noted sadly, hadn't seemed to notice at all.

Lori seemed to sense what Gayle was thinking. "I used to think it was pretty lonely to be in the house while my mother was working on one of her cases," she said. "It's almost like she's not even there, locked up in her study. But at least she makes the time for me when I need it. I wish there was something I could do to change things for you."

Gayle looked at her friend in amazement. "Don't you realize how much you've already done—just by being my friend? I've never had anyone I could share my feelings with, the way I do with you. No one else has ever understood."

"I could say the same thing," Lori added.

For several long moments Gayle looked across at her friend and then back down at the table, trying to decide whether she should say what was on her mind. But before she opened her mouth, Lori broke in.

"I recognize that look on your face, Gayle. I ought to. We've both got the same problem, bottling up what we're thinking, instead of sharing it with someone else. It's taken me a long time to realize I have friends I can talk to and confide in. I want you to think you've got one, too."

"I know. That's why I was wondering if you had something you wanted to tell me."

Lori looked genuinely puzzled. "No. Like what?"

"Bruce told me you called him your boyfriend."

"Oh, that!" Lori laughed. "We were just having fun—at least I thought we were. He doesn't think I'm really interested in him that way, does he?"

Gayle shook her head. "No, he's still pining after Cheryl. I just didn't want you to get hurt again if something didn't work out."

"Like with Chris?" Gayle knew it still pained Lori to talk about her relationship with Chris Farleigh, a man twelve years her senior, whose adult responsibilities were too much for her to handle. Lori had shied away from starting a new relationship with anyone since then, and Gayle had been reluctant to bring up the subject, afraid of dredging up feelings that Lori would rather have remain buried. "I've learned my lesson, Gayle," she said quietly. "However, I don't think Bruce is my type."

"Do you think he's Cheryl's?" Gayle wondered.

Lori shrugged. "Maybe, when we're done with him..."

Gayle decided to speak out. "Well, I don't. And to tell you the truth, I'm not so sure that Operation Superhunk's such a good idea, either."

"I had my doubts too, when we started, but I think we've done Bruce a favor. He doesn't look so out of place now."

"I'm not really talking so much about the clothes, or even my teaching him how to drive. I'm happy to do that, it feels good to help someone. It's the concept of molding his personality to suit us that bothers me," Gayle explained. "It's as if everyone has decided that Bruce should be turned into their ideal, perfect boyfriend. Kit's trying to make him as good a dancer as Justin. Alex wants him to play tennis as well as Wes. Elaine's trying to make him into the social charmer she'd like Carl to be. Stephanie's turning him into someone as cool as..."

"Rick Forrester," Lori completed.

"She likes Rick?" Gayle asked, surprised. "Anyway, as far as Bruce goes, I don't see what's wrong with him the way he is."

"I'm inclined to agree with you. He's got a funny sense of humor, and I find his awkwardness endearing in a way. But right now he's too rough to attract someone as sophisticated and demanding as Cheryl, and at least he's smart enough to see he'd have to change to make her notice him. All we're doing is helping him out."

"I hope we're not making a mistake," Gayle said. "I'd hate to think we're really like Dr. Frankenstein, creating our own twentieth-century monster."

Two days later Gayle ran into Ginger on the cafeteria line. She and Craig were eating together and invited Gayle to sit with them out on the lawn.

"How are the driving lessons going?" asked Ginger after they parked their trays under the shade of a large cottonwood tree.

"Fine. He ought to be ready for his road test sometime next week. How's the dancing?" Gayle responded.

"Great, though sometimes I think the two of us are a bit much for him," she said.

"I don't know, sounds like hog heaven to me." Craig smiled.

"You can come over and join us anytime, Bo Jangles," offered Ginger. "Actually, I think Bruce is making great progress. Kit's a wonderful teacher and Bruce may actually have some hidden talent—though right now he moves more like a wooden soldier than Barishnykov." She then went on to tell Gayle about what had taken place during the first lesson a few days before. "He stepped on Kit's toes enough to make her black and blue for years. Kit told him there was a certain grace in the way he did it, though. At first I thought it was a little mean of Kit to tease him like that, but it turned out to be a good thing. He got over his shyness real quickly and forgot about Kit as a girl and just treated her as a teacher," Ginger said. "Underneath that mask of anxiety he's got quite a sense of humor."

"Gee, maybe I should look into some of that teacher stuff, too," Craig said.

"As long as I'm the teacher," noted Ginger, giving his tennis shoe an affectionate kick.

Gayle felt a little uncomfortable for Bruce, maybe even a little jealous that Kit could affect him so easily. Well, he was certainly getting a quick initiation. He'd be ready for Cheryl a lot faster than he knew.

A few days later Gayle ran into Bruce and Stephanie after school. Bruce was dressed in new, better-fitting Guess jeans and a sleeveless sweat shirt he wore reversed. He also had on a pair of wraparound shades, which made him look a little like the guy in the Calvin Klein billboard on Glenwood Drive. Gayle was intrigued. So was Celia Borden, who walked by and flashed a smile his way.

Stephanie had on a short black leather jacket, a tight jeans skirt, and a cotton T-shirt with the words THE BEST MAN FOR THE JOB IS A WOMAN. Stephanie also had on sunglasses. She was trying to teach him about what was cool and what wasn't.

"The important thing is to know what is cool, right?" Stephanie asked, welcoming

Gayle into the group as if she were glad to get some help.

"Well, I guess. I mean it depends," Gayle answered vaguely as she joined them.

"Porsches are cool," Stephanie continued, ignoring Gayle's equivocal response. "So is any European car, except for Volvo's—unless it's the 1800. Datsun Z's are dogs. Any old American car, if it's cherried out, is good to be seen in, too. You've got to dance, but break dancing is gone. It's history, except for the moon walk."

Bruce tried to take it all in, but he was having trouble following her rapid-fire delivery. So, too, for that matter, was Gayle.

"Smoking is definitely not cool. But if you quit smoking, that's admirable. I quit," she said proudly.

"Was it hard?" Bruce asked.

"Yeah, but I did it. Do you two smoke?" she asked both Gayle and Bruce.

"No," they both answered.

"Good, that makes it easy for you. What else is cool, Gayle?" she asked.

"Eddie Murphy?" Gayle offered.

"Super," Stephanie said emphatically.

"What about the Cubs?" asked Bruce.

"Never heard any of their albums, who are they?" puzzled Stephanie.

"No, they're a baseball team," he said, sounding surprised she didn't know.

"Sports, huh? I don't know. You'd have a hard time convincing me sports are cool. Of

39

course, Alex would disagree with me on that. Mainly, I think sports are fun. Anyhow, do you think you get the picture?"

"No," was his honest response.

She shrugged. "Well, we'll work on it another time. I've got to go," she said, noticing someone crossing to the far parking lot. She hurried over there. Gayle thought it might be Rick Forrester, but she wasn't sure.

"How's it going?" asked Gayle, amused, turning back to Bruce.

"Not so good. I think I've got geek in my blood," Bruce confided with a smile.

"Don't be silly. Stephanie's not the authority on everything," Gayle encouraged him.

"It's not that. It's just that I'm not sure all this cool stuff is the real me," he said, distracted.

"I think I know what you mean." She hesitated, unsure as to how to bring up the subject. "Are you...uh, having any luck yet with Cheryl?"

"Fortunately, I don't have time to dwell on her, especially since I have a feeling she doesn't think much of guys from Chicago. In fact, I doubt she'd even think *about* a guy from Chicago at all," he said. "She still walks by me as if I didn't exist."

"Maybe that's her way of flirting with you," Gayle said, trying not to sound too cynical. "You know Cheryl, she's used to guys pursuing *her*." But when Gayle saw the despondent look on Bruce's face, she quickly added,

"Don't give up, though. If you really like her, I'm sure she'll come around." Gayle was immediately rewarded with a smile.

"I've got to run, now. Tennis, this time with Craig. See you at the next driving lesson," he called out to her as he hurried away to join Craig, who was waiting near the courts.

Gayle walked slowly to her car, replaying the conversation in her head. She kept getting stuck at the part about Cheryl, feeling badly because she had not been honest with Bruce. Deep down inside, she was glad Cheryl was ignoring him. Glad, because she wanted the best for Bruce, wanted him to be happy, and she didn't believe Cheryl Abrahamson could give him that happiness.

Chapter Four

A few days later Gayle, Lori, and Stephanie were sprawled out on the wide campus lawn after school, taking advantage of an unusually warm springtime sun. They were discussing the upcoming Senior Impersonation Night. The annual affair featured a variety show followed by a dance, the admission ticket to which was a costume depicting a famous person.

"Who are you going to be, Stephanie?" Gayle asked.

As if in defiance of the sun, Stephanie was lying on her stomach, her head resting between folded arms. "I don't know yet. I suppose I could always show up as James Dean in *Rebel Without a Cause*."

"You're supposed to come in costume, not

your usual clothes," Lori said. The blonde cast a critical look at Stephanie's black leather vest and matching knee-high leather boots, which she wore over a pair of skin-tight blue jeans. "Hey, aren't you hot with all that stuff on?"

"Nah, I never sweat," Stephanie said. "So who are you going to impersonate?"

"I don't know yet," Lori said, tilting her face to the sun. "I haven't been struck with any inspirations. All I know is that Kit's going as Shirley Temple. She's doing a dance routine, naturally. What about you, Gayle?"

Gayle didn't know what to say. She hadn't thought about going until now. "Mmm," she responded, dreamily. "Who would I like to be? Someone glamorous, sexy, alluring..." She glanced mischievously at Lori. "Marilyn Monroe?"

Lori sat up abruptly and stared at her friend. "Wow, you've come a long way to be able to suggest that. Now, if only you'd do it!"

"It was just a joke," Gayle protested.

"But seriously, Gayle, you've got a nice figure now," Lori pointed out.

"Don't be afraid to show it off," Stephanie added.

Gayle was silent for a moment, then said shyly, "What about this blouse?" Unconsciously she fingered the collar of her new green checked shirt. "I picked it out by myself the other day. I think it's the first thing I've bought that you didn't help me with."

44

"It's a step in the right direction. But I think it would look even better if you did this." Lori sidled over to Gayle and unfastened the top two buttons. She also rolled up the long sleeves, exposing the gentle line of Gayle's long, slender arms. "There, that's better," she said.

"Hey, you're right," Stephanie observed, seemingly amazed at how the simple changes suddenly emphasized the flattering curves of Gayle's body. "You're a miracle worker, Lori," she said, sitting up. Then, looking beyond the girls she added, "Speaking of which, here comes your latest project. Wow."

Gayle turned around and saw Bruce walking out the front door. She had to agree with Stephanie's assessment. Dressed in a gray corduroy shirt with the sleeves rolled up, black denim jeans, and gray running shoes, Bruce had a casual, yet purposeful air about him. It was evident in the new spring in his step, too. She noticed that two sophomore girls practically dropped their jaws as they watched him walk by; apparently, in their eyes, he already was a hunk. Gayle had to admit he looked great, except for the final cap to his look—those black, wraparound sunglasses. She didn't like the way they hid his hazel eyes and the way they sort of crinkled up when he smiled.

Lori said, "My first impulse was to dress him in really wild clothes, to make him stand out. Then I realized that would work against

45

his personality. He'd feel too uncomfortable dressed in something loud and garish, and that would defeat the purpose of everything, right? So I opted for something simple yet stylish."

"He's not getting lost in the crowd anymore," Gayle said, noticing another underclassgirl stopping to give him the once-over.

Bruce noticed his friends, waved, and hurried over to them. "I've had enough of this place," he said, dropping to his knees next to Gayle. "Ms. O'Neill gave us a pop quiz—for which I was unprepared, naturally. I really sweated bullets waiting for the bell to ring." Turning to Gayle, he asked, "Do you think you could give me a ride home, Gayle? I don't feel like dealing with the bus."

"Sure," she said, "I was just about to leave anyway."

"Uh, by the way, that's a nice blouse," he added.

"Thank you." Gayle wasn't sure if he really meant it or was practicing one of Elaine's techniques, but she liked hearing him say it just the same.

As the four of them headed toward the parking lot, Gayle noticed Bruce's attention focused on the crowd in front of them. With those sunglasses on, she couldn't tell what he was looking at—that is, not until Cheryl Abrahamson crossed the path right in front of them. She was with another cheerleader, Roseanne Parker, and their eyes darted between the sidewalk and the copy of *People* in Cheryl's hand.

Bruce smiled. "Hi, Cheryl," he called.

Cheryl looked up briefly, then returned her eyes to the magazine.

Even under the sunglasses Bruce appeared crushed. His whole body language changed, and he began to walk with his head bent down. Gayle's heart went out to him, knowing all too well about the terrible pain of rejection. She turned toward Cheryl to give the insensitive blonde a glare of her own. But to her surprise Cheryl had done a double take and was now staring at them—or, more specifically, at Bruce. Cheryl whispered something to Roseanne, and while Gayle was too far away to hear, she saw that Bruce's "crush" was smiling.

Gayle didn't have time to tell Bruce about what had happened because just then Lori cried out, "What's going on over there?" A small crowd had gathered around a fancy red car in the parking lot.

"I know! That must be Rick Forrester and his new Ferrari." Stephanie perked up. "I'd heard a rumor he got one from his father for his birthday, but I didn't believe it. What a car!"

"A snob car, you mean," Lori said.

"Hey, Rick's not a snob," Stephanie said, quick to jump to his defense. "It's not his fault he's rich. He doesn't flaunt his money the way some people around here do. He says it's no

47

big deal."

"How can you call a Ferrari no big deal?" Gayle wondered.

"I didn't say *I* felt that way," Stephanie explained.

As they joined the admiring crowd, Gayle noticed that Stephanie seemed to be paying as much attention to Rick as she was to the car. What a romantic match they'd be, she thought—two people from such different backgrounds. Of course, right now, she thought *any* couple was romantic.

"I've never seen a car like this. How fast can it go?" Bruce asked Rick as he walked around the front to the driver's side.

"About a hundred and forty," Rick answered, looking slightly awed himself.

"How fast will *you* go?" Bruce continued, peering inside to look at the dashboard.

"Oh, about as fast as I can get away with," Rick responded casually, leaning up against the hood. Rick Forrester didn't need lessons in how to look right. The tall, lean senior had curly chestnut-brown hair that framed a ruggedly handsome face highlighted by wide, soulful eyes the color of melted chocolate. As he rested against his new car, Gayle was struck by his understated outfit of jeans and a T-shirt. Anyone else dressed like that would be considered a slob; yet, somehow, on Rick the clothes took on a neat, but casual, dimension.

Everyone laughed at Rick's remark as they wandered around the bright red car. Stephanie moved a little closer to Rick, pretending to look into the back window but keeping her eyes glued to him.

"How can you drive it at night? It doesn't have any headlights," Bruce wondered.

"Hey, Bruce, wake up. Everybody knows the answer to that," Rusty Hughes, a football player not exactly known for his intelligence, remarked from the crowd.

But Rick didn't think the question was stupid. He reached into the car and pulled a lever. The headlights appeared. "See? They turn up."

"Oh, yeah. I just forgot," Bruce mumbled. It was a small, insignificant mistake, but Gayle could see that Bruce was embarrassed. Immediately he went back into his shell. It didn't matter to him that no one made a big deal out of it, and that, in fact, a lot of the others were glad to see Rick demonstrate the lights. Bruce drifted off to the side, his hands in his pockets and his eyes to the ground.

In the quiet that followed, Stephanie piped up in an uncharacteristically nervous voice, "I like the way it looks, like a futuristic car or something from the movies."

Gayle could see that Stephanie was trying as hard as she could to make Rick notice her. "I've never seen her act this way around a guy before," she whispered to Lori, who nodded conspiratorially.

"Yeah, it looks like a James Bond car. Which is probably somewhat silly here in

Glenwood. I just hope I don't wreck it," Rick said.

"Do you think he likes her?" Gayle asked Lori.

"At least he's talking to her," Lori replied. "He may be more of a human being than I've given him credit for."

"You must feel pretty lucky," Stephanie said to Rick.

He glanced around as most of the crowd drifted off. "To tell you the truth, Stephanie, I'm a little embarrassed. I wanted a car, but I sure didn't expect one like this. I don't think you'll catch me giving it back, though." He laughed.

"I don't blame you," Stephanie said, as she grew visibly more relaxed.

"Hey, would you like to go for a ride? I could take you home," he asked.

Stephanie looked as if she might faint right there on the tarmac. She turned to Gayle and Lori with eyes as big and bright as the Ferrari's headlights.

"Sure, I'd love to—if it's not too far out of your way," she answered, turning back to Rick. She appeared so weak kneed that Gayle was afraid she might collapse before stepping into the car.

"Let's take the long way around, through Stanford, and break it in," he said quite casually as he moved to open the door for her.

As they drove off, Gayle and Lori let out a chuckle.

"Boy, we'll hear about this ride for the next week!" Gayle said.

"But first I've got to study. See you later," Lori said, as she shouldered her books and headed to the library on the far side of the parking lot.

That left Gayle alone with the nearly forgotten Bruce. She noticed he had put away his sunglasses and was waiting quietly for her off to the side.

"Gee, looks like I lost my other passengers," Gayle said. "That means you get to sit in the front with me."

Gayle meant the remark as a joke, but to her, Bruce still looked upset. She wanted to tell Bruce she didn't think he had made a fool of himself, but she held back.

As they got into her VW, she noticed his expression had changed. Now he had a faraway look in his eyes. That, at least, was something she could identify with.

"Thinking about your old school back in Chicago?" she asked, as they drove off.

"Yeah, how'd you guess?" he answered.

"I recognized the look. I used to think about my old school a lot. I don't do that very often anymore," Gayle explained.

"But you haven't forgotten your friends in San Francisco have you?"

"No," she answered quickly, trying to blot out the ugly truth that she hadn't had any friends to forget. Just then she heard Lori's admonition in her head, *"Don't look back-*

ward. Think only about the good things waiting in the world for you." "It's just that I've made new friends here and am happier now. You know what I mean?" she added, not at all sure she did herself. Until she'd said the words aloud she hadn't realized she felt that way.

"I think I do. But there are some things I miss. Like going down to Old Town with the guys on the weekend. Playing ice hockey in Lincoln Park—"

"You ice skate?" Gayle asked, amazed.

"I'm not Wayne Gretzky, but I have a good time—or should I say, used to. I think what I'm really going to miss the most, though, is spending Saturday afternoons at Wrigley Field."

"At least you can still see the Cubs when they play at Candlestick," Gayle noted. "Imagine how much worse it would have been if you moved to someplace like Seattle or Kansas City."

"American League cities," Bruce said, chuckling. "How come you know so much about baseball?"

"You're looking at a hopeless Giants fan," she said.

"I'm glad I found someone who understands baseball," he said approvingly.

"I'm strictly an observer. I don't even play softball—or at least not very well," Gayle confessed. "But I love to go to the games, eat hot dogs and peanuts, cheer on my favorite players..." Bruce chuckled.

"So what do you miss the most about your old school?"

"I guess I'd have to say my photography class. I had such a good teacher—he was a real photographer."

"I had the same sort of teacher in my astronomy class. He really made it interesting, because it was more than a job for him. It was his life," Bruce said. "By the way, how about showing me your shoebox camera and your photos? You promised you would."

Automatically, Gayle started to say no, but forced herself to stop. Again she could hear Lori's words of encouragement, *"Be proud of your achievements, Gayle. You have nothing to hide."* And curiously enough, she had to admit she wanted to show the photos to Bruce.

"Oh, all right. But you have to promise not to laugh at them. You're the first person at Glenwood I've ever shown them to," she said, feeling nervous but excited.

It wasn't until they arrived at her house that it suddenly struck her she would be all alone with him. Her experience with boys was so limited she had no idea what it might mean. Bruce seemed nice, but the idea of being alone with him in the house made her nervous.

"My dad's probably golfing and my mother's at her restaurant. We can look at the photos out on the patio," she said as she hurried up to her bedroom to get the shoebox camera and her photographs. Somehow, she felt that being outside was safer.

When Gayle sat down on the bright yellow lounge chair, she put the photographs on the glass-topped table in front of her and waited for Bruce to pull up a chair. But he didn't. Instead, he sat down beside her on the cushion. Gayle swallowed, feeling herself blush; his knee was warm and nice next to her bare leg. Suddenly, she felt surprisingly light-headed. *It must be because I had so little lunch*, she told herself.

"Here it is," she said out loud, holding up her homemade camera, nervously searching his face for a reaction.

It was a regular shoebox covered with black tape and reenforced on the bottom and one end.

"It looks like a mini submarine," he observed.

"I told you you'd make fun of me."

"No, I'm not. It just looks so solid."

"It's really very simple. All cameras are essentially just like this one—even the most sophisticated ones work on the same principle. They're just more fancy," she began, showing him the inside of the shoebox.

She held up the holder for the film plate for him to look at. He reached out to touch it, and as he did their fingers brushed briefly. Gayle felt the same unexpected thrill she remembered from the day she taught him how to shift. The gesture caused her to loosen her grip on the holder, however, and it fell on the brick patio floor. Bruce picked it up for her and as he handed it back she noticed that his fingers were trembling slightly. What was going on? Had he felt it, too?

"Uh, that's basically it," she said, keeping her eyes focused on the camera. "You just have to expose the film for a long time, because you aren't letting in very much light. It might take anywhere from one to five minutes," she concluded.

"Really? That long? Let's look at these pictures you brought down," he suggested, sounding so genuinely interested in the photos that Gayle lost her feeling of uneasiness at being alone with him.

"Sure, here." She handed him a few while she continued to talk. "These have a special 'style' to them. They are kind of soft focus and splotchy, with fuzzy edges. But sometimes that is just the right effect."

As Bruce looked over the three or four photographs in his hand, a sudden, cool breeze coursed through the patio, tousling his neatly combed hair. "I've never seen anything quite like them. They're great. Really great!" he exclaimed.

"You think so?" Gayle responded. A thrill ran up her spine, but Gayle didn't know if she was reacting to the compliment, the new chill in the air, or something about the way Bruce ran his fingers through his hair to comb it back into place. He didn't quite succeed—one errant lock fell over his left eye—but the look made him look somehow vulnerable...and appealing in a way Gayle didn't quite understand.

She tried to focus on the pictures, but they couldn't hold her attention. Out of the corner of her eye, she glanced at Bruce. His face had color—the beginning of a tan—probably the result of his hours on the tennis court. His jawline was strong and in the light, it looked set, in a determined sort of way.

All of a sudden, he turned, startling her as he caught her staring at him. For a moment, neither spoke. Gayle felt as if she were frozen in time.

He handed her one of the pictures. It looked like a young woman on a very bright beach sunning herself next to some rocks. The girl had long hair and was posed in such a way that it was unclear if she had on a bathing suit or if she was nude. Everything was in soft focus and very luminescent.

"It's really neat, like a dream of a beautiful woman. Is that you in the shot?" he asked.

"Me?" she replied, somewhat amazed. A beautiful woman? Did Bruce really think she was pretty? "Oh, no, it's not me. It's—it's one of my old dolls."

"A doll? How could it be?" he asked, puzzled.

"I shot it right here in my room. Well, actually in my bedroom at my old house. It was easy. The waves in the background are from a poster. But the rocks are real. Then I placed the doll in the middle of all of that and turned off all the lights, except for one little one, which I shined right on the doll."

"Wow, it looks so real! Why did you use a poster for the wave?"

"It took five minutes to expose the film. No real wave will stand still that long, so I had to use a picture so I wouldn't get a blur."

"Yeah, of course. That's really neat, Gayle. You're very clever," Bruce said. Gayle didn't stop to wonder this time if that was just a line from one of Kit's flirting lessons. Now she really wanted to believe he liked her pictures and appreciated some of the effort behind them. She wasn't sure why, but it was important to her to have his approval.

They were so engrossed in the pictures that they had failed to notice that evening was coming on and a thunderstorm was on the horizon. It was one of those quick-mounting Bay Area storms that swept in from the ocean, dispensed its rain, and moved on. The first flash of lightning and subsequent thunder startled them out of their discussion of the photographs.

"Oh, great! A thunderstorm! I've been wanting to take a picture of a lightning bolt for a long time," Gayle exclaimed.

"Can I watch?" Bruce asked, walking out to the edge of the patio to look at the darkening skies.

"I can't take it from here," she said, fretting. "You have to leave the shutter open, and if there is a lot of ambient light around, you don't get the shot."

"I see. It's just like that with telescopes. You can see more when they're up on mountain tops and don't have to fight the reflection of city lights in the atmosphere," Bruce said. "So why don't we drive up to the mountains? You ought to be able to get a great shot there."

"We'd have to hurry," Gayle said, not daring to believe they were really going to do it.

"Great, let's get going then. I'll drive. You get your camera ready while I'm at the wheel. That'll save time."

"But you don't have a driver's license," she pointed out.

"Who cares? This is art." He laughed. "Besides, I've had enough lessons to pass the test. You know I can drive."

"Okay, let's go!" cried Gayle, swept away by the urgency of the storm.

Racing up the stairs to get her equipment —the Nikon, tripod, film, and special shutter cable—Gayle felt a surge of adrenaline course through her. Like a little kid promised a ride on a Ferris wheel, she scrambled eagerly to collect her things, not even fully aware of what excited her so. She felt wild and adventuresome, fearless and invincible, and as she hurried out of her room, she caught sight of herself in the mirror.

Her face was flushed, her open eyes shining, and her red mane of hair was tousled by the wind, falling down around her shoulders in masses of curls. She paused, taken aback by the vision of what looked like a lovely girl in the mirror. She hadn't taken a photograph since she'd moved to Glenwood, and it felt good to be doing it again. But something more than the thrill of photography had stirred inside of her. It was the thrill of being alone with Bruce.

Chapter Five

"I feel like Benjamin Franklin! Racing into the stormy, primitive mountains in the name of science and art, in search of the elusive Great Pumpkin." Bruce laughed as he guided Gayle's old VW up into the mountains.

Gayle was hunched over her photographic equipment trying to get everything ready. "I think you've got things a little mixed up, Bruce," she deadpanned, although the grin on her face betrayed her delight.

"You drive, I'll navigate. Just follow this road," she told him.

"Right," he said.

Gayle paused from attaching her camera to the tripod and looked at Bruce, who was staring intently at the storm up ahead. He really seemed to be caught up in the excitement of chasing a lightning bolt as if it were as important to him as it was to her.

He glanced at her, and quickly she looked down at her camera, afraid that he might have noticed that she had been staring at him. What they were doing was crazy, she thought, yet she had no desire to turn back. With each passing moment she was feeling more and more alive. Why hadn't she ever been this impulsive before? She was definitely entering unchartered territory, and the relentless pounding of her heart told her the reaction was not limited to the quest for the elusive lightning bolt.

"There's the state park sign," he said, spotting it up ahead.

"Turn in there, I think there is a little hill nearby where we can set up the camera." Gayle instructed him.

They turned into the wooded park and drove on. Under the dark, brooding sky, Gayle noticed the park had a rugged, wilderness feel to it. It was hard to imagine, here among the tall sequoia trees, that a few short miles away over a million people were crowded into the valley below. Gayle felt as if she were entering another world, one that exhilarated her and one in which she could be a whole different person.

"It sure is dark up here. Kind of eerie," Bruce remarked, as they snaked their way along the wooded lane.

"But there's no ambient light to ruin the

shot," she responded, trying to keep her mind concentrated on the task at hand.

Lightning suddenly struck up ahead and thunder closely followed. It began to sprinkle.

"There, that's the place. Pull in over there!" Gayle exclaimed, seeing a small clearing on a knoll up ahead.

Bruce parked the car next to the grassy knoll. The little hill was elevated enough so that there was a clear view of the sprawling Coast Range to the north.

There was a sudden flash of lightning, and the mountains were briefly lit up by the harsh light. The thunder followed a few counts later.

"Wow, we're right in the middle of the storm now!" Bruce shouted over the thunder.

"This is the perfect place. I just hope we aren't too late. Let's go!" she said, gathering up all her gear.

Before she could finish her sentence a deluge of rain came crashing over them. "Oh, no, will the rain ruin the picture?" asked Bruce.

"Not if we keep the camera dry, but maybe we shouldn't try," she said cautiously, trying not to feel disappointed.

"Are you kidding? I didn't come all this way for nothing. I don't care if I get wet. Do you have an umbrella? I'll hold it," he offered.

"In the back."

"Don't worry, it'll work," he said. Hurriedly Bruce tried to pull the umbrella out from the back seat while he stepped out into the rain.

In his excitement, he accidentally opened the umbrella before he got out of the car. By the time he got through wrestling with it, he was thoroughly soaked. Ignoring his own discomfort, he hurried around to the other side to open the door for Gayle.

"Oh, Bruce! You're all wet," Gayle said.

"Don't worry about me. Just make sure you and the camera stay dry," he reassured her.

Gathering up her equipment, she stepped out of the car under the umbrella he held for her. It was raining and the wind was blowing pretty hard, but Bruce huddled close to her as they walked up the grassy knoll. The closeness was creating a tension in Gayle that would have been unbearable if she hadn't had the photograph to concentrate on. She looked around trying to figure out which would be the best spot to place the camera. Finally she selected a spot near the top of the knoll.

"Is there anything I can do to help?" he asked.

"Believe me, holding the umbrella is a tremendous help," she said as she quickly set up her collapsible tripod and arranged the camera. Bruce kept the umbrella over her as she worked.

"But how can you get an image? There's hardly any light," he shouted above the storm.

"I'll leave the shutter open, and the very small amount of light will slowly expose the film. Then, hopefully, a lightning bolt will strike where I'm pointed," she shouted back.

"What if it hits us?" asked Bruce.

She laughed. "I don't think it will. Those trees are up much higher than we are."

There was a short pause as they both shifted a little under the umbrella.

"You sure know a lot about this, Gayle. I'm impressed," he said, in an altered voice. He looked intently at her, trying to read her expression in the dark.

Gayle didn't answer him. She felt both hopeful and yet strangely scared. Turning away to the camera, she was afraid to reveal the confusing emotions inside her. For a brief moment it had appeared that he liked what he saw when he looked into her eyes. Another ripple ran through her body. Could Bruce be thinking of her, in that way? The same way she was now thinking about him? It was dark, and she couldn't really read his expression. Part of her was too afraid to find out.

Yet the rain, if anything, was heightening her attraction to him. All rain soaked and windblown, his long, dark eyelashes were stuck together with little beads of water like points of a star. She could see a flush on his cheeks that made him look robust, a solidity and strength to his face that the storm seemed to accent. Right now, with the cold air around them, she could feel the warmth of his body, a warmth that drew her closer to him.

Gayle wondered what he thought of her. She knew he had said he had a crush on Cheryl, but was it possible that he could be interested in her now? Her heart wanted to say yes, but her mind told her she was reading too much into the situation. Cheryl was beautiful, flashy, and popular. Next to her, Gayle felt like a nobody.

Still, she couldn't resist taking another look at Bruce. He was gazing at the sky, searching for the next lightning bolt. A drop of water momentarily hung from his chin like a jewel, before it fell. They were standing very close huddled under the umbrella. She accidentally brushed against his shoulder, and he glanced down at her.

"I'm sorry," he apologized. "I didn't realize the umbrella wasn't covering you. You're getting wet."

"Oh, don't worry about me. Just as long as the camera doesn't get soaked. Besides you're pretty wet, too," she responded. His thin windbreaker had long ago gotten soaked all the way through. But then she could feel that the yellow cotton sweater she'd thrown on hastily before they'd left was not much drier.

"Oh, you know us superhunks—we never feel the cold," Bruce joked in a falsely hearty voice. "But, you know, Gayle, I feel like we're about to discover something—that we're participating in something wonderful and magical."

"Really?" she asked, hoping against hope he meant it in the same way she did.

"Yeah. This is really an amazing storm. I'm glad I'm here," he said, looking just a little

66

unsure of himself.

"So am I. I'm glad we decided to do it," she said in a slightly awkward voice. "Even though I didn't realize how cold it would be. I'm freezing."

Nervously, Bruce moved his feet up and down for a moment and looked away. In a slightly awkward motion, he reached around and lightly put his arm over her shoulders.

"Just to keep you warm." He smiled.

This time, the "look" was in his eyes, she was sure of it. His arm felt nice, although she wished he would rest it on her a little more. It felt like a feather.

"That's nice, it feels warmer. Thanks," she said.

He relaxed a little more and *really* put his arm around her. Her heart began to race, and a funny feeling swept through her body, leaving her knees slightly weak and spongy.

The fury of the storm mounted with every beat of Gayle's racing heart. The rain fell heavily all around them, cutting them off from the rest of the park like strings of glass beads. With Bruce's arm wrapped around her, Gayle could feel the rise and fall of his chest. It excited her, and her heart beat faster. She couldn't tell what was louder, the pounding rain or her pounding heart.

Then he shivered, and she turned and met his eyes. He appeared altered in some way, as if he were older or had suddenly grown very serious. Slowly, almost as if he were hypnotized, he moved his other arm to her side and tilted his head toward hers. His eyes were soft and inviting, his face was so close that she could feel his warm breath. A thrill ran through her body like an electric shiver. Oblivious of the cold and the wet, she was only aware of Bruce before her. Of Bruce leaning down to touch her lips with his...

She half-closed her eyes in anticipation as he bent to kiss her. Suddenly the sky was lit up by the flash of a lightning bolt striking very close by. The nearly immediate and deafening roll of thunder was so loud it almost knocked them over.

They both jumped apart, as startled by what they had almost done as by the thunder. Jarred back to reality by the rude timing of the thunder, Bruce turned away, as if regretting his attempted passion. Gayle turned to check her camera.

"Gosh, that was close!" Bruce exclaimed.

Gayle still faced the camera, trying to compose herself. She was too choked with unfulfilled desire to speak.

There was a long pause before Bruce managed to ask, "Do you think you got the picture?"

"I hope so," she said disappointedly as she looked at the sky. "Because it looks like that was our only chance." *Let him think I'm disappointed only about the storm*, she thought to herself.

Already Gayle could see the sky clearing in

the west. The storm was losing steam rapidly, as if the lightning bolt had been its final act of fury before passing on. They stood there, at a loss, watching, while the rain eased quickly to a fading sprinkle, and the wind tapered down to a gentle breeze.

Bruce was the first to recognize that the umbrella was no longer needed and began to close it up. Almost, Gayle thought, as if he wanted to avoid thinking about what had started to happen between them. So she busied herself with her camera, and neither of them said anything. From Bruce's behavior she could conclude only that his had been a passion brought on by the storm's intensity, an irrational impulse to join with nature and abandon himself to the tempest. She didn't think she could bear to hear him tell her it had all been a mistake. Even though she'd lived through seventeen years full of rejection, this was one brush-off she knew she wouldn't take lightly.

"Kind of strange how quickly the storm passed," Bruce offered. "Back in Chicago we'd get some monster storms that'd go on for hours."

"Thunderstorms out here are like that," Gayle answered as she finished with the camera.

"We might as well go back to the car," he offered reluctantly.

"I suppose so," she agreed.

Her disappointment was evident in her

voice. Her mind was racing, imagining what might have happened if the thunder and lightning had come only a few seconds later. They might have created a little spark of their own, one that could have ignited into...

Gayle still wasn't sure. Bruce had been just a friend before tonight. She had never thought of him as a boyfriend, and she had no way of knowing how he felt. Besides there was Cheryl, and she was crazy to think she had a chance against a girl like her. But it had been romantic. For one brief moment, a boy had wanted to kiss her. And even if the very lightning bolt they'd sought had taken him away from her and ruined it, she'd still have that knowledge in her heart.

Chapter Six

"It's a flower."

"No it's not, it's a wave breaking on the sand."

"It *is* water, but I think it's a fancy fountain."

"Let me see it," said Elaine, taking the photograph Kit and Lori had been examining.

Elaine walked across Gayle's large bedroom to get a better look at it in the bright Saturday afternoon sunlight. She wasn't wearing her contacts, so she pulled her glasses down on her nose and made a show of studying the unframed black-and-white print. Gayle nervously fidgeted with the waistline of her faded blue jeans, as she leaned against the wall near the window, waiting for Elaine's verdict. Finally, Elaine turned to her audience, addressing them over the top of her glasses in

71

the mock snooty voice of an expert.

"You're all wrong. You don't have any taste. Anyone with the artistic sense of a baboon can see it's a picture of a . . . of a . . . What is this, Gayle?"

Gayle had been afraid of this. The minute she found out that Bruce had told Lori about her hobby, she knew her new friends would want to see her photographs. Actually, she was flattered they were interested, but she still got nervous about showing them the pictures. She was worried that—somehow— if the girls didn't like them, they wouldn't like her. She knew it was silly and irrational, but she couldn't help herself.

"C'mon, Gayle, what is it?" Lori insisted.

"It's a close-up picture of two seashells. They're on a piece of butcher paper with light shining on them from underneath. It didn't quite work," she answered, a little embarrassed she had to explain it.

"Seashells? Of course! They're wonderful!" exclaimed Kit, snapping her fingers in recognition, as she examined the print again.

"Gee, Gayle, you've really got something here," said Elaine, who was now sitting on the bed next to Lori. "I also like this one with the girl on the beach. People should see these."

"I agree. I can't imagine anyone not liking them," Lori insisted, rising from the bed to her full height with one of the pictures in her hand.

"No, this is just a hobby for me," Gayle

72

insisted.

"Why not show them around and get some opinions?" asked Lori.

"I'd die of embarrassment," exclaimed Gayle.

"I've got an idea," interrupted Elaine, refusing to give in to Gayle's reluctance. "The Street Fair is coming up pretty soon, and they have prizes for all sorts of crafts, including photography. You should enter them and see if you get a ribbon."

"You owe it to the rest of us ungifted slobs to show your talent for all to see," Lori added.

Gayle looked at her best friend and smiled. Leave it to Lori to make her see how childishly she was reacting. She had to admit that at times she, too, had thought about entering some of her photographs in the contests she always read about in her photo magazines. She had just never had the courage to do it. The thought of opening up her private little world to the opinions of total strangers was terrifying. But now, with her friends' support...

"Okay, you win. I'll look into it," Gayle agreed, relieved in a way that they'd forced her to make a decision. "But now that we've got that out of the way, let's get on with the real reason we're all here!"

"Okay, everybody, progress reports," announced Elaine. The girls quickly found spots around Gayle's spacious bedroom. Elaine opened up a notebook she'd brought along and began to speak.

"It seems obvious that Lori's had the most immediate success. Just by changing Bruce's clothes you've already made him *look* like a superhunk," she said. "By the way, maybe you could do something for Carl. His wardrobe could sure use upgrading." Elaine laughed.

"Now that you mention it, Justin could use a few pointers on his clothes, too," Kit chimed in.

"C'mon, you too. Justin and Carl are just fine the way they are. You're both luckier than you admit. Bruce just needed to get clothes that are more suited to California," said Lori.

"I was surprised how quickly he learned to dance," Kit added. "He's surprisingly good at spins and turns. The guy's got great ankles."

"That's from his ice skating," Gayle piped up.

"He never told me about that," Kit said.

"Uh, we had a lot of time to talk during the driving lessons," Gayle said, hoping the flush of embarrassment she felt inside wasn't making her blush. She hadn't told any of the girls—not even Lori—about her burgeoning feelings for Bruce. She'd especially kept quiet about the storm. She wanted to cherish the memory of what almost happened that day, without having to hear an analysis of "why it just wouldn't work" or "but you know he likes Cheryl...." Besides, since then Bruce, while friendly, had acted as if it had never happened. Now she, too, was beginning to wonder if it hadn't just been a strange and wonderful dream.

"So when do you think he'll be ready for his test?" Elaine asked, her felt-tip pen poised on her note pad.

"He's already got an appointment scheduled for next Saturday."

"Good," Elaine said, marking that down in the pad. "He's getting better at strategy, too. Yesterday, I suggested he practice approaching girls by asking Christina Ferrel for a homework assignment. At first he got mixed up and asked her for the English homework, even though it's physics he has with her. But he didn't let it bother him — in fact, he joked about it. I tell you, considering we bombarded him from a lot of angles, I think he's turning out all right."

"Well, I think it's time for his coming out party," Kit said. "I vote we go to Flips in Palo Alto next Friday night. It's a great place to dance."

"I second the motion," Lori said.

"Do you think we should work out a plan to somehow get Cheryl there, so he can dance with her, too?" asked Elaine.

"No, definitely not. Bruce told me he didn't want to go anywhere Cheryl might be, because he still feels he needs practice and doesn't want to blow it the first time out. Besides, I found out she'll be out of town next weekend," explained Kit.

"Perfect," responded Elaine.

With the mention of the blond cheerleader, Gayle withdrew from the conversation. While everyone else began to discuss what they would wear and who they would try to get to come, Gayle worried about Cheryl. Just yesterday she saw her chatting with Derek Johnson during lunch, huddling next to Ben Price in the school library, and, though she'd never reveal it to Stephanie, poised next to Rick Forrester's Ferrari after school. Cheryl seemed to be everywhere the boys were—all the boys but Bruce, that is—and yet, was she as far out of Bruce's league as they had originally thought?

"I think Alex and Wes will definitely come," Kit was saying as Gayle turned her attention back to the conversation. "Ginger and Craig, too."

"Carl and I will come. I think I can actually get him to dance, too," Elaine said.

Gayle realized unhappily that most of them had dates already planned for that night, whereas she would be going alone. Only Lori, Stephanie, and she didn't have anybody to go with and Stephanie didn't really count. She obviously had her eye on Rick Forrester, and she was such a good dancer and looked so good in heels, that the guys always stood in line to ask her to dance.

Gayle would go with Lori. After Lori and Chris Farleigh had broken up, Lori had stopped dating for the time being. Gayle felt it would be a good break for her friend to just have a pleasant, unpressured evening dancing.

It wouldn't be that easy, though, she thought to herself. She had no idea what to expect. When she had been fat it was easy—she knew to expect nothing. But now? Though the other girls didn't realize it, this wouldn't be just Bruce's coming out dance. It would be hers, too.

Chapter Seven

Gayle couldn't believe her eyes. Or her ears. This was the first disco she'd ever been in, and she felt as if she had been submerged in a whole different set of physical sensations. The sound was incredibly loud and it came from everywhere, wrapping around her like a liquid blanket. Colored lights lined the ceiling, the dance floor, and even the multicolored carpeted couches that surrounded the floor on three sides. The intense colors didn't burn or twinkle, but flowed around the disco in pulsing waves, in time to the music. The effect was so seductive that she began swaying to the relentless beat of the music as soon as she stepped onto the disco's shiny black floor.

"This is some place!" Gayle exclaimed.

"I know. Isn't it amazing!" Lori gushed. "I

just love the neon couches. What do you think, Bruce?" she asked, turning to face him. The three of them had driven there together in Lori's car and had planned to meet everyone there, but for the moment they couldn't see their friends. They gravitated to one of the few vacant couches in one corner of the disco.

"I'm not sure I'm ready for this," Bruce said finally, eyeing the swarm of bodies already jammed onto the dance floor. Gayle thought she detected a fleeting look of terror in his eyes. She figured he probably felt enough pressure just dancing for the first time, let alone dancing in a place that looked like the inside of a giant jukebox.

Gayle then wondered if she was merely projecting her own worries onto Bruce. The place *was* intimidating, at least at first. Scouting the girls around her she was seized with a momentary fear that her deep green silk T-shirt dress was all wrong for this place. Not that she didn't think it made her look pretty. Her black leather belt helped accent her ample curves and gave her legs a long, slender look, and the dress was the perfect color to go with her red hair. But everyone else seemed to be dressed far more outrageously, in dresses that just barely covered their backsides or form-fitting slacks that looked as if they were practically painted on.

Lori seemed to sense Gayle's doubts in the way only a best friend could. "Gayle, you look perfect in that dress. It really makes you stand out," she said looking Gayle over.

"Thanks—" Gayle murmured, thankful for the encouragement. "I only hope I look half as good as you do."

Lori was wearing a tight, shiny dark blue dress with a deep slit up one side and high heels. Her long blond hair was up in a loose chignon, and she looked as regal as a princess.

"You look so pretty the boys probably won't let you off the dance floor," Lori chided her.

The hard pounding music magically shifted to a quieter ballad-type song. Scanning the dance floor, Gayle spotted Kit and Justin waving to them. She noticed that Kit, no stranger to Flips, fit in perfectly. She was wearing pink shoes and white bobby socks, a very short pleated white skirt, a skimpy, pink, spaghetti-strapped blouse, and pink earrings the size of silver dollars. Gayle thought she looked stunning. Then again, she thought, Kit would look sexy in a potato sack.

Stephanie came around the corner from the coat room and hurried up to them. "Have you seen Rick? When we went for that ride in his Ferrari he said he sometimes comes here," she bubbled eagerly to the two of them.

"No, we haven't. But it's early yet," offered Lori.

"Yeah," Stephanie said, looking around.

Stephanie had known what to expect at the disco and had dressed for it, Gayle noted.

Decked out in over-the-knee boots, a short pale blue skirt with two overlapping hip-belts, and a tiny blue blouse that flattered her figure nicely she looked, as she liked to put it, fit to kill.

Gayle sighed to herself. Why did she have such gorgeous friends? She was afraid no one would ever ask her to dance.

Gayle stared out at the dance floor, but instead of seeing the flashing neon lights her mind saw a roomful of multicolored balloons. She was back in the gym at her old junior high school, the night of the end-of-the-year eighth grade dance. She hadn't wanted to go, in fact would have been content to spend the night watching the Giants on TV, but her mother had insisted on it, telling Gayle that the only way she'd ever rid herself of her anxieties was to confront them head on. In fact, her mother had gone to the trouble of fixing her up with Gaylord Fitzpatrick, one of her friends' sons. Like Gayle, he had the dubious distinction of being the fattest person in his class.

Gayle had tried to prepare herself by learning how to dance. When her sister and brother-in-law had come up from San Diego for a visit, Gayle had asked them to teach her how to fast dance. But their dancing evolution had ended with The Hustle so they weren't much help, though they did teach her how to do a simple box step.

As it turned out, her preparations hardly

mattered, since the night turned out to be the biggest disaster in Gayle's life. Klutzy Gaylord had been just as nervous about dancing as she and opted to spend the evening standing next to the snack table, munching from a seemingly bottomless bowl of potato chips. But Molly Singer, one of the popular girls in Gayle's class, had been intrigued with the idea of seeing them dance and had egged them onto the floor. Gayle could still hear the giggles of Molly and her friends as they had watched her and Gaylord wriggle their hips and step on each other's toes. She imagined they must have looked like a couple of bumper cars and had been so embarrassed she had run off the floor to the snack table as soon as the music had stopped. And poor Gaylord had only managed to make things worse. In his effort to cheer her up he'd handed her a glass of punch — in the process spilling it all over her dress.

Gayle shook herself, bringing the neon lights back into focus. *I've got to stop tormenting myself like this*, she wailed inwardly, reminding herself that that had been the old, fat Gayle, the Gayle who no longer existed. She was no longer a bad dancer, either. After that awful night she had begun watching *Dance Fever* and, in the privacy of her bedroom, had taught herself how to move gracefully. The aerobics class she was taking with Lori had also improved her skills. True, she'd never tested herself on a real dance floor with a boy, but, on the other hand, there was no better time to try than right now.

It was then she decided she'd ask Bruce to dance with her. She realized he, too, was nervous about his skills and would probably appreciate getting his feet wet with someone who wouldn't want to dance circles around him, like some of the show-offy girls she now saw on the floor. Summoning up her courage, she twisted her body on the couch to face him.

But he was gone. So was everyone else, she realized with a jolt. Quickly she spotted Lori out on the dance floor with a Glenwood junior whose name she didn't know. Stephanie, Kit, and Ginger were out there, too, along with some other faces from Glenwood she recognized. But where was Bruce?

She tried to quell the strange feeling of jealousy that was beginning to well up inside her as she concluded he must have asked someone else to dance. Then magically Bruce appeared in front of her, holding out a drink.

"Diet 7-Up?" he asked, handing the glass to her.

"Thanks," she said, impressed with his thoughtfulness and secretly happy he wasn't dancing.

"I overheard you telling Lori you were on a diet. I don't know why, though," he said, taking a sip of his cola. "I think you look great in that dress."

"I see Kit's taught you well," she said.

"Yeah—come-on line number six," he said,

grinning like a pleased little boy. "But I really mean it."

"I like your tie," she offered.

Bruce was wearing black denim jeans, leather shoes, and a white dress shirt with rolled-up sleeves. The fashion touch was the bright blue, burgundy, gray, and yellow striped tie. It added just enough color to give him a rakish, punkish air.

"You do? I thought Lori had lost her mind, but I guess it fits in here. I'm lucky she didn't insist I wear an earring to match."

"If you change your mind, you can have one of mine," Gayle said, pointing to her green lacquered hoops.

"No, they clash with the tie." Bruce put his index finger over his lip, the way Lori did whenever she was pondering a clothing match.

Gayle recognized the gesture and smiled. "Gee, you ought to go to Senior Impersonation Night as Lori."

"Me? I haven't even thought about going. Anyway, I heard you're supposed to dress up as a famous person."

"Well, Lori's going to be famous. I just know she'll be a fantastic model."

"You'll get no argument from me there. But if I go, it'll be as a famous male. No way I'll ever wear a dress." Bruce took another sip of his soda, then turned to Gayle. "Do you think you're brave enough to risk my first dance?" he asked.

"Ah, so you're eager to plunge into the fray," Gayle teased.

"With you at my side to guide me, I know I'd never take a false step," Bruce bantered, setting down his drink and holding out his hand to Gayle.

"Great, this song is one of my favorites," she said, trying to sound casual but wishing desperately that she had half the dancing experience Bruce obviously thought she did.

Bruce led her to an open spot and began easily to dance. Right away Gayle concluded Kit must have been a good teacher, because he looked relaxed and confident. Bruce did a quick side step and a couple of spins that were as good as any she'd seen on *Dance Fever*—and a lot better than most of the guys around them.

The song ended just as Gayle was really getting into it and, for a moment, she stood awkwardly next to Bruce, wondering what she should do. But before she could move, Bruce gave a slight shrug of his shoulders as if to ask for this dance, too, and Gayle nodded readily. It was a slow dance, and the lights dimmed as Bruce took her into his arms and began to move with even more confidence. Gayle had never dreamed dancing with a guy could be so harmonious. He really knew how to lead and give support without crowding her. She began to get a little more creative in the turns he initiated, at one point letting her arm fly out effortlessly like a graceful bird wing.

"Hey, I like that," Bruce said. "You're actually good."

"No, you are," she said. "I'm just reacting to your cues."

Bruce held her closely again, so close that Gayle could rest her cheek against his chin, taking in the spicy yet comfortable aroma of the cologne he was wearing. A tingling sensation danced over the surface of her skin. She hardly knew what music was playing as she concentrated on the warm glow she felt being close to him. She held her breath as if to savor the excitement. Dancing with Bruce was the most natural thing in the world; they belonged together, and she wished the song would never stop. But, all too soon, it did.

For a brief moment they remained in each other's arms as if both had been listening to their own rhythms and not the music's. Gayle glanced into his eyes and, awkwardly, slowly drew away from him. She realized she was trembling. They stood there for a moment, staring at each other, and still Bruce said nothing. Then finally, he spoke.

"Thanks for the dance."

Gayle smiled, waiting for him to guide her to the couches or maybe buy her another drink. But he had something else in mind.

"All of you girls have been so great to me, I really don't know what to say—except I'd better get on with it," he mumbled. "Wish me luck, Gayle."

"But..." The words stuck in her throat as she watched Bruce walk away, seemingly gaining confidence with each step, as he headed for the sidelines to ask other girls to dance.

Left alone on the edge of the dance floor, Gayle felt as if she'd been kicked in the stomach. She'd been so happy dancing with him—it was devastating to think she'd been nothing but a guinea pig for him. Hadn't he felt *any* of the tremors of excitement she'd experienced while in his arms? Obviously not, she concluded as she saw him escorting Cheryl's best friend Roseanne onto the dance floor.

I hate you, Bruce! Gayle said to herself, half wanting to run back to the dance floor and punch him in the nose for making her feel so miserable. But instead, she drifted over to the couches and retrieved her drink.

Her friends weren't even there to commiserate with. Lori was still dancing, this time with a blond guy who looked old enough to be a Stanford student. Alex and Wes were talking on a couch up in one of the darker areas. She waved to get their attention, but they were so involved with each other they didn't notice. Kit and Justin and Ginger and Craig were dancing, as was Stephanie who, with Rick nowhere in sight, had latched onto a lanky, redheaded guy in a Sunnyvale High sweat shirt. Only Gayle was without a dance partner, and she was about to resign herself to another long and lonely evening of sitting on a couch sipping too many Diet 7-Ups and trying to look unconcerned.

Then she stopped herself. If Bruce could be out there having a good time, then so could she! She'd show him he wasn't the only boy in town. No sooner had she begun to scan the room when she made eye contact with a dark-haired guy with a bushy mustache. Instead of averting her eyes as was her habit, she forced herself to keep her gaze on him, adding a smile to help entice him over. It worked, and a few seconds later he asked her to dance. He looked a lot older than even the few college-age guys there, and as he led Gayle onto the dance floor, a strange, new excitement flushed her cheeks. An older man! She never could have dreamed this up.

He never did tell her his name, but Gayle didn't mind. He was a good dancer, and she found herself having fun. After a few dances she thanked him and returned to the side-lines, feeling, somehow, it was unwise to dance too often with someone so obviously older than she. She knew from Lori's experience that she'd only be asking for trouble.

No sooner did she get off the floor than Mark, a guy from her Spanish class, asked her for a dance. She was surprised to see him there, having figured him to be an all-books, no-party type. Mark wasn't an accomplished dancer, but he was an enthusiastic one, and they had fun talking. He had come with friends, and one of them quickly led her back to the dance floor almost before she could thank Mark.

As the evening progressed, Gayle spent more time on the dance floor than not. She had long ago lost track of her half-finished 7-Up. She had never danced so much in her whole life! It was fun, but somehow not as exciting as she had imagined it would be. No matter who she was dancing with, she'd find herself looking around to see what Bruce was doing. It was ridiculous! He'd made it clear she was only a friend to him, that he was more interested in testing his new-found social skills with other girls. In a way, she couldn't blame him. Who wouldn't want to be more popular and attractive? Bruce looked so confident and flirtatious that Gayle wondered if their plan to create a superhunk had maybe succeeded too well. Had some of the most charming aspects of the old Bruce gotten lost with the emergence of the new Bruce? All at once, Gayle realized she didn't want him to change—she didn't want him to get all popular and caught up in Cheryl's crowd.

When Mark asked if she needed a ride home, she gladly said yes. Gayle knew it was just a friendly gesture, but that was fine with her. At least one boy had cared enough to ask.

Chapter Eight

The smell of frying bacon was enough to make Gayle sick, but she stood determinedly over the kitchen stove early the next morning. She used to love that smoky aroma, but now that greasy foods like bacon were on her forbidden list everything about it was distasteful to her. She made a quick check of the eggs, poaching on the range to her right. So far, so good, she remarked to herself, as she turned her attention to the bread slices she was about to pop into the toaster oven. There was a time when she used to make a breakfast like this for herself every Saturday morning; but this meal wasn't for her, it was for her parents.

Gayle could hear them walking around

upstairs, getting ready for the day that lay ahead. She knew they'd be surprised to find breakfast waiting for them. Usually they were in too much of a rush to fix anything more than toast and coffee.

Her father was the first to appear, dressed as usual in his yellow golfing cardigan and yellow, black, and beige windowpane pants. His full head of hair had long ago whitened from the deep red color Gayle had inherited. "Good morning, Gayle," he said, giving her a perfunctory kiss on the cheek before picking up the morning paper from the kitchen counter. "Is that bacon I smell?" he asked as he sat down at the table.

"With poached eggs and toast," she said proudly. "Do you want anything in your coffee?"

"Just black, dear," he said, already lost behind the business section.

As Gayle served her father, her mother came into the kitchen. In her typical whirlwind fashion, Gayle noticed she was attaching a gold braided earring to one ear as she scurried to the table. "You're such a dear to make breakfast this morning," she told Gayle. "But hold the bacon. I'm on a diet."

Aren't we all, Gayle wanted to add. She had deliberately put on one of the first pair of jeans she'd bought when she started losing weight. The waist was so loose it was practically hanging around her hips. She was hoping her mother would notice and decide today was the day she'd take her into San Francisco for her long-promised shopping spree.

"Did you see this, Lorraine?" Mr. Rodgers lowered his newspaper enough to point to an article he was reading. "Gold is up again. I told you we should have bought those futures contracts."

"I still say it's a bad investment. The stock market's the place to be now."

Gayle sat down next to her mother, behind a small bowl of cottage cheese and fruit, as her parents debated where to invest their money. Although they were hardly as rich as the Forresters, they had more money than they knew what to do with, as far as Gayle was concerned. She just didn't understand what all the fuss was about.

She toyed with her breakfast, playing with her spoon as she thought about the other reason she wanted to go into the city with her mother. She was awfully confused about what had happened—or, more accurately, what hadn't happened—at the disco. The strange feeling that had come over her when she'd been dancing with Bruce, how it felt so different from dancing with the other boys. The jealousy she'd felt when she saw Bruce with other girls—all this was new to her, and even though she'd never discussed things like this with her mother, she wanted to very much. Wasn't that what mothers were supposed to be for? Still, she worried about how to broach the subject and felt that it would be easier to do so in the more impersonal atmosphere of a San Francisco store.

Her parents continued to talk business throughout breakfast, forgetting their daughter was even there. Finally, Gayle got tired of playing with her unwanted food and rose to rinse the bowl in the sink. Then, as she bent down to put it in the dishwasher, her jeans slipped below her hips, exposing half her backside. With an astonished gasp, Gayle hiked them up, but not before her mother, at last, noticed.

"Gayle," she cried out. "Don't you have anything better to wear?"

"Well, I've been losing more weight..." she began.

"Look, take some money out of my purse and go shopping today with your friend—uh—what's her name?" Mrs. Rodgers left the words dangling in the air.

Her mother became a blur as Gayle felt her eyes moisten with tears. "It's Lori," she said, trying to hold her emotions in check. "But, Mom," she added, summoning up all her courage, "I'd really like to go shopping with you."

"You know I'd love to, dear," Mrs. Rodgers said, "but I can't today. I've got a meeting with my chef at one."

"We could leave now," Gayle ventured.

"But how would you get home?" her mother countered. "We'll go some other time. I promise."

Gayle wanted to say she could take the bus or a taxi or they could drive separate cars into the city, but she didn't bother. From previous experience she knew her mother would come up with one excuse after another why she didn't want her around. "Sure, some other time," she said, the disappointment heavy in her voice.

"Hey, don't look at me," her father added, trying to make light of the situation. "I've got about as much clothes sense as that frying pan over there." He rose from his chair and headed toward the garage. "And I've got a threesome to meet in ten minutes. See you later, everybody." With a quick salute he was gone.

Her mother left several minutes later "to take care of business" before her one o'clock meeting. Gayle wasn't sure whether to believe her or not. But in the end it didn't matter; once again she was all alone on Saturday morning.

She stared at the empty kitchen in a bleary daze. She really didn't want anything to eat, but there wasn't anything else to do. In the past the temptation to fill her loneliness with food had usually won out. She decided she'd better give Lori a call before this craving got out of hand. Lori had told her to call any time of the day or night whenever she got an irresistible urge to, as she put it, pig out.

She hurried upstairs to use her own bedroom phone, but before she could get there it began to ring. Probably Lori calling, she thought—just one more proof of the way they seemed to be able to read each other's thoughts.

"How did you know I just came from the refrigerator?" Gayle blurted out. "It was carrot sticks, I swear, but boy am I glad you called, Lori. I'm so depressed about last night, I was just about to..."

"Lori? I'm sorry, maybe I have the wrong number. I'm calling for Gayle..." a male voice tentatively offered.

"Oh, my goodness! Bruce! I'm sorry, I thought you were Lori. I mean, I was expecting Lori to call and..." Gayle wanted to scream with embarrassment—she was so shocked to hear Bruce's voice that she jumped off the bed, nearly bumping her head on the ceiling. The phone clattered to the floor.

"What's going on there? Are you all right, Gayle?" Bruce asked.

"Oh, yeah, I'm fine. I'm sorry. I dropped the phone. Just a minute, let me get settled here," she stuttered and stammered. With a hand over the receiver, she took a few deep breaths and tried to calm herself. Geez! She had nearly told Bruce how she secretly felt about him! How could she have been so dumb? She had to change the subject! But what *was* the subject!?

"Maybe this isn't a good time to call, Gayle. But I just wanted to let you know the good news," Bruce began.

"Good news? What is it?" Gayle asked,

thankful that he didn't seem to notice she was acting like a total idiot.

"I passed my driver's test. I can now legally drive in the state of California," he said proudly.

"That's wonderful, Bruce. I knew you could do it!" Gayle exclaimed. Then she added in a different tone of voice, "I suppose that means you won't be needing lessons anymore."

"Yeah, but I couldn't have done it without your help. You were a great teacher."

"Thanks. I enjoyed it, too."

"By the way, Gayle, I've been meaning to ask you. How did that picture of the lightning bolt turn out?"

"Oh, it's great. We got lucky."

"And awfully wet. But it was one of the neatest evenings I've ever had. I'd love to see it," he said, sincerely.

Gayle shifted uneasily on the bed. The memory of that night in the storm had a sad aura to it for her, especially after last night at the disco. She didn't know how to respond to his curiosity about the picture.

"I'll bring it to school on Monday," she offered.

"Hey, why wait? I can drive over there. Now that I've got my license I should use it, don't you think? That is, if you're not too busy?" he added.

"No, of course not. I mean, yes, you can come over," she began to stammer again. "But what are you going to drive?"

"My mom's car. I can't wait to get behind the wheel of a car with nobody in it but me!" He laughed.

Gayle barely had time to change into a pair of burgundy cords and a white Esprit sweat shirt and drag a comb through her hair before Bruce arrived. She had splashed her face with cold water and put on a little mascara, but he didn't seem to notice. He was anxious to see the photo, so she showed him.

"It's great," he said. "It really is. I like the way the rolling hills in the background seem to be lit up by the lightning bolt."

"Yeah, that does look nice. I'm just glad it struck where it did" she added.

"It's funny, but it doesn't look very wet—all I remember is getting soaked." He laughed.

"We sure did. Rain is hard to photograph, though, especially with an open shutter," she explained.

"This is so good I think you should enter it in that Street Fair Elaine was talking about," Bruce suggested.

"Oh, she told you about that?" Gayle asked.

"Sure, and I think it's a great idea. That picture of the doll on the beach would be so great. You're really talented, Gayle, you should try it," he said, his eyes sparkling as he looked at her.

"Thanks. But I don't know. I don't have them mounted or framed...and you have to frame them to enter them," she said, searching for excuses.

"I could help you with that. I'm pretty good with my hands. I built a telescope, after all," he reminded her.

Gayle hesitated. Bruce seemed so full of confidence and energy. In addition to getting his driver's license that morning, he was obviously also basking in the success on the dance floor. Gayle deliberately left that subject untouched. Right here, alone with him, it was easy to pretend Cheryl and all those other girls didn't exist. She wanted to believe he'd come here not just to see the photo, but to see her, too. "Okay," she said, hope rising within her. Maybe by the time they completed the framing Bruce would have asked her out. Their first real date.

At the frame store, Gayle was impressed with the way Bruce handled himself. He was so handsome and confident, asking lots of questions as they carefully selected the right matting for each picture. He also was very patient when she took a long time to pick out a frame for the lightning bolt photo.

"The key to framing a picture is not so much what you show as what you don't show," she explained when they returned to her father's workshop to begin the work. "We'll just get rid of the wasted space with the matting. On the doll picture it's just the opposite. We want the soft focus—the fuzzy edges—to show. It adds to the mood of the whole shot."

"I see what you mean. It's like you're fine

tuning the original photograph, getting a second chance to frame what you were after when you made the shot," he responded.

"Exactly! You don't always get it right the first time. But if you take the time to think about what you're doing and what you want, you can eventually get it right."

"Boy, there sure are lots of times when I wish I had a second chance on things. It's so easy to flub the first time around."

"I know what you mean. But everyone does that," she said, thinking about the disco.

They were quiet for a while as Gayle set up the framing materials. She wondered what Bruce had been thinking about when he mentioned second chances. But glancing over at his intense hazel eyes as he studied one of the photographs, she felt tongue-tied.

It took them a full two hours to frame just three pictures: the two seashells, the doll on the beach, and, of course, the lightning bolt. Those were the only ones she wanted to enter.

"I just hope some people enjoy them," she said, as she propped up each one on the workbench so they could look at them.

"I can't make up my mind. I like them all. No matter how hard you try, you won't get me to pick a favorite," he told her.

"I won't. You're supposed to like all three."
"Good."
They both laughed.

"This has been a productive morning, I really enjoyed it," Bruce said. "But you have to promise me one thing."

"What?" she asked.

"That you'll let me show you my telescope. You still haven't seen it," he said.

"I'd love to. You know I like astronomy," she readily agreed. Her heart pounded quickly, in anticipation of Bruce's next words. He *was* going to ask her out!

"I'd invite you tonight, but my folks are having some friends over ... and I have to be there, and all," he explained.

"That's okay. Some other time," she said, trying to hide her disappointment.

"Well, I guess I'd better be going," he said quietly. He didn't appear to really want to go, yet he seemed to think he'd better. He was acting a bit strange, and Gayle sensed something was on his mind.

"Well, if you ever need a favor ... or ... or ... anything, don't hesitate to ask," she offered genuinely.

Bruce paused for a moment. There was a strange look on his face as he struggled with what he wanted to say.

"Well, there is something. Sort of, but I'm not sure if I should ..." he finally said.

"Go ahead, ask. Anything," she said, encouraging him. *Don't be afraid to ask me out.*

"Well, after we spoke about Senior Impersonation Night I started to do some thinking. I've really started to like dancing and I was wondering ... You see, I have this idea for a Fred Astaire and Ginger Rogers dance

101

team . . ." he stammered, sounding as shaky as the old Bruce.

Gayle's heart jumped into her throat. He was going to ask her to be his partner. It was the most exciting thing that had ever happened to her. The Impersonation Night was one of the biggest events of the year. But before she could jump in and tell him she'd love to go, he finished his request.

". . . and I was going to ask Cheryl to be my partner, but I'm scared I might ruin it. I was wondering if you could find out if she might be interested. I know it's a strange request, but you've been such a good friend and all. I'd really appreciate it," he stumbled on, looking very relieved that he had finally gotten the words out.

Gayle couldn't believe it. For a moment, she was too amazed at the audacity of his request to feel anything. Then the hurt set in, and it took every ounce of self-control she had not to reveal what she had been hoping. How could he do this to her? But she didn't dare let Bruce know how she felt. She couldn't stand it if he felt sorry for her. She managed to get control of her voice and answered him.

"Sure, Bruce. I can try and find out. I have a PE class with her," she said, as calmly as she could.

"Oh, that's great. Don't, you know, let on that I might ask her. Just, like, get an idea if she might want to do that," he babbled on, relieved he had an ally in Gayle.

"Oh, I bet she would," she assured him.

After he had left, her calm facade collapsed under the burden of her anger and hurt. Bruce was completely blind to her! All he saw was Cheryl. To make matters worse, now she had to be their go-between! How could things get so mixed up?

Chapter Nine

Dressed in a white skirt and a bright yellow sleeveless blouse with one button daringly left open, Gayle walked along the sidewalk to the gym that Monday morning. She lingered there, letting the warm spring sun fall on her bare arms. If she didn't hurry she was going to be late for PE, but she didn't really care.

Gayle had never liked PE. When she had been heavy, it had been the one place in school where she came face-to-face with her weight problem. The physical exertion was always too tiring and taxing for her, yet she hadn't minded that as much as the snickering and staring from her much thinner classmates.

Even now, despite having lost so much weight, she still felt insecure about putting on her Glenwood gym shorts. No matter how hard she tried she still pictured the other girls giggling behind her back.

And today was going to be even worse: Bruce had given her the horrible job of speaking to Cheryl Abrahamson. Normally, Gayle never would have considered it. The rich, curly-haired blonde was one of the most popular girls at school—and one of the snobbiest. The way she looked at her, Cheryl still made Gayle feel as insignificant as a piece of lint on the floor. As the double doors to the gym came into her sight, Gayle wondered if she could stage a sudden fainting spell—just to avoid having to go to class that day.

As she turned into the gym, someone called out behind her. "Hey, Gayle, you're going to be late for class."

It was Derek Johnson, a blue-eyed, shaggy-haired blond boy who had a reputation for moving fast with girls—*very* fast. Kit had told her to watch out for him, a warning Gayle had laughed about at the time. She still found it hard to believe that any boy would go out of his way to talk to her, although she *had* danced with a lot of guys at the disco....

Gayle turned to Derek. "Oh, it's only PE," she told him, managing a small smile.

"Yeah? I never liked PE either, though I would change my mind if they made it co-ed. How about you?" he asked, looking at her with a strange mix of curiosity and humor.

"I don't know about that," she hesitated,

surprised at his boldness.

"Think about it. Well, see you around," he said giving her the once over with his eyes.

Gayle was shocked speechless. She felt a blush rush to her cheeks, but the final bell came to the rescue and she hurried into the gym.

Sitting down next to her secluded corner locker, she began to undress, still dazed by the brief encounter. Derek flirted with lots of girls, but only cute ones. The thought that he might find her attractive thrilled her, even if she didn't really like aggressive guys like Derek.

The problem is, she reflected as she gazed at her image in the locker room mirror, my body looks so grown up—under control—but inside I feel so confused.

Gayle arrived on the gym floor just as Cheryl and Marcia Connors were beginning to pick teams for volleyball. Gayle knew she had to get on Cheryl's team to do Bruce's favor. But how?

A moment later, in what seemed to Gayle an act of divine intervention, Cheryl picked her for her team.

Gayle felt she had to make the most of the opportunity, so she stood next to Cheryl while they warmed up with some stretching exercises. "Uh, thanks for asking me to be on your team," she said.

"I've been meaning to for a long time," Cheryl responded, as she touched the floor with the flat of her palm. "I couldn't help but notice you've lost some weight lately. How'd you do it?"

Cheryl was asking *her* a question? "A lot of carrot sticks—and a roll of tape to keep my mouth shut," she said with a chuckle, feeling flattered. They talked a little while longer, and Gayle was surprised at how friendly and amiable Cheryl seemed.

Just as the game was about to start, Cheryl said, "I bet now that you're thin, you're getting a lot of attention from boys."

"I wish," Gayle said, thinking of Bruce. "Not really," she added.

The two girls lined up next to each other beside the net. As their teammates took their places, Cheryl asked, "What about that new guy, Bruce Fletcher? Haven't I seen you hanging out with him after school?"

Gayle was so shocked by the question, she failed to react when the ball came over the net right at her. It hit her on the leg and bounced under the net. "Sorry," she whispered to Cheryl.

"Who cares?" Cheryl shrugged. Gayle was surprised: Cheryl was being awfully nice to her. "So tell me about you and Bruce," she continued.

"There's nothing to tell, really. We're just friends. I taught him how to drive..."

In between serves Gayle found herself telling Cheryl almost everything she knew about Bruce—that he was from Chicago, that he loved to ice skate, had built his own telescope... Everything, that is, except how she really felt about him.

"When he first came here I thought he was kind of dumb. But I guess I was wrong, huh?" Cheryl said as she rotated positions. "Roseanne danced with him at Flips on Friday. She told me he's a cool dancer."

"Yeah, that's because—" Gayle stopped herself. Bruce would die if she told anyone about Operation Superhunk. "—he really knows how to move."

"Score one for him," Cheryl said, as she got ready to serve. After she sent the ball sailing in a perfect arc over the net she added, "And you don't have anything going with him?"

"No," Gayle said sadly.

But Cheryl didn't pick up on Gayle's regretful tone. "That's all I wanted to know." The smile was a dead giveaway that Bruce's efforts to improve himself hadn't gone for naught. Cheryl had noticed him—and apparently liked what she saw.

For the rest of the game Cheryl ignored Gayle's attempts to continue their conversation. Gayle grew increasingly angry as she realized what had really happened: Cheryl hadn't turned on the good buddy routine because she wanted to become her friend—she was just pumping her for information about Bruce.

Although this meant she'd accomplished her mission for Bruce, Gayle wasn't happy about it at all. At that moment she hated

Cheryl, hated the cocky look on her face that said, "Bruce, here I come," as if he'd melt in her arms as soon as she gave the word. The worst part was that she knew Cheryl would get exactly what she wanted. Gayle dreaded having to tell Bruce the "good" news.

As soon as she walked into history class, Gayle could see that Bruce wanted to know if she'd been successful. It was written all over his face. But Gayle was so upset she wouldn't look at him and made him wait until the end of class to find out.

When the bell rang she bolted from her seat, eager to escape the tension and pain she'd felt all period. But she didn't get far before Bruce stopped her, grabbing her shoulder and pulling her to the side of the hallway.

"What's the rush?" he asked, a new hard, demanding tone in his voice. "Didn't you do what I asked you to?"

"Of course I did," she said.

"So what happened? What did she say?"

The combination of Cheryl's insincerity and Bruce's insensitivity made Gayle explode. "You want to know? You really want to know?" she taunted him. "I hardly had to try. She asked about you right off the bat. I'm sure she'd love to go out with you."

"Fantastic!" Bruce clapped his hands with joy.

"Yeah, terrific," Gayle said sarcastically.

"Hey, what's wrong? Aren't you happy for me?"

Gayle wanted to tell him the truth, that Cheryl used people and spit them out when she was through. But she'd done him enough favors. Let him find out the truth himself—the hard way. "Oh, yes, Bruce I *am* happy for you. Happy because you're going to get everything you deserve," Gayle shot back. "Why don't you go out and have a terrific time with Cheryl—you two deserve each other."

Gayle wanted to take back the words as soon as she said them, but when she looked at Bruce she saw he hadn't even detected any sarcasm. *How thick-headed can you be?* she thought, hysterically.

"Well, I will," Bruce replied, a little puzzled but obviously not too bothered by Gayle's outburst. "See you." And he headed for the door at the end of the hall.

A voice jangled Gayle out of her thoughts.

"Hey, Gayle. Could you give me a hand?"

It was Mark, the boy she had danced with at the disco. He was about to put up a poster announcing Senior Impersonation Night.

"Oh, sure." She smiled, as she held the poster up so he could pin it to the bulletin board.

"Last year's was really fun. You gonna go?" he asked.

"Maybe. Just to watch," she said cautiously.

"If I had the guts I'd go as Bozo the Clown and spray everyone in the audience with seltzer." He laughed as he finished tacking up the poster.

111

"You wouldn't!" She joined his laughter.

"Yeah, you're right, but I sure would like to do one crazy thing before I graduate. Anyway, I'll see you at the show, okay?"

As they hurried down the hallway, Gayle felt a little better. Maybe there were more fish in the sea than she realized, she thought.

And just maybe she'd do something about it.

Chapter Ten

"Hello."

"Hi, Gayle. This is Bruce."

"Hi," was her guarded response.

"Listen, I was wondering," he said casually. "It's a real clear night and I've been wanting to show you my telescope for the longest time. Why don't you come on over?"

She paused before she answered. Should she say she was busy? But she really didn't want to do that. She could no more reject an invitation from him than forget to breathe.

"Sure, Bruce. I'm not doing anything right now, anyway," she added at the end to protect herself.

"Great! I'll pick you up in a half hour," he said, sounding genuinely pleased.

"That's okay. I'll drive over. It's no trouble,"

she said.

If she drove over she thought it would feel more like a friendly visit and less like a date—which, she firmly reminded herself, was just the way she wanted it.

A little while later, Gayle found herself at Bruce's front door, rapping on the old-fashioned brass knocker and admiring the stained-glass inlays on either side of the weathered oak entryway. The two-story neo-Victorian house was in one of the older sections of Glenwood, and to Gayle's mind it had much more charm than her parents' ultra-modern house.

A freckled-faced boy answered the door. "Whaddya want?" he asked bluntly.

"I'm here to see Bruce," she said.

"Come on in. I'll get him," the boy said, opening the door for her. "Hey, Bruuuuuce," he shouted, as he ran down the hall to the kitchen.

The first thing that hit Gayle was the noise. From the doorway she could see two small boys sitting in front of a television set with the sound turned way up. From someplace upstairs she heard Twisted Sister's latest song and the shuffle of feet moving around the floor. The living room to her left was scattered with playing cards, Gobots, and the remnants of a race car track.

Gayle chuckled to herself. Her mother would have a stroke if she had to deal with a mess like that. She hated to see anything out of place and was constantly nagging Gayle to hang up her clothes practically the minute she took them off. Gayle liked all the clutter and noise—it gave this house life.

The boy who had let her in came back with a somewhat pudgy woman, whose short brown hair was streaked with gray. "Hi, I'm Bruce's mother," the woman said, smiling, as she wiped her hands on an obviously well broken-in apron. "You must be Gayle. Bruce told me you were coming."

"Nice to meet you," Gayle said, shaking Mrs. Fletcher's outstretched hand. She wondered how much Bruce had told his mother about her. How much could he tell her?

"He's out in the back. Let me show you the way." Mrs. Fletcher walked Gayle through a spacious wood-beamed kitchen fragrant with the aroma of baked goods. She opened the door that led to the backyard, where Bruce was busily setting up his telescope. "If you two get hungry, just come in. I'm baking a fresh batch of cherry pies."

Gayle smiled and thanked Mrs. Fletcher before heading outside.

Bruce's house was built on a small ridge with the backyard looking out over Glenwood and the valley. The mountains were visible in the distance, and Gayle was reminded of the day the two of them had driven up there and come so close to sharing something special.

"You built that?" she asked, eyeing the telescope.

"Yeah, a few years ago—took me all summer," he said proudly. "Why don't you take a look."

Gayle put her eye up to the telescope.

"I've got it pointed at Orion right now. It takes a moment for your eye to adjust," he explained.

"I can see it! It's so close! Wow, it looks amazingly bright and clear," she exclaimed excitedly. "Let's look at something else."

"Like what?" he said.

"I don't know. How about Venus?" she suggested, pointing to the lower part of the sky.

"Great!" he said.

Bruce went on to show her how to move the telescope with the various cranks and wheels. Gayle was fascinated and had a wonderful time panning across the sky looking at the various stars. She could tell Bruce appreciated her understanding of astronomy, too. Somehow she couldn't quite picture Cheryl getting as excited about seeing Jupiter as she had been. After looking at quite a few different constellations, Bruce asked, "Why do you like it?"

Gayle paused for a moment. He was looking directly into her eyes, a gaze that made the surface of her skin tingle.

"It's hard to say, really. I guess because it's so mysterious. We don't know what's out there and...and...there are so many possibilities," she began.

"Do you think there is life out there?" he asked.

"I hope so. When I look at the sky and see all those stars I get this strange feeling of hope and, like, awe. I mean, somebody might be looking back at us." She was becoming entranced by this quiet, clear night. Impulsively, she slipped off her sandals, feeling the cool grass beneath her feet. Somewhere in the distance, she heard music playing. Probably from a stereo inside. Even though she and Bruce were just in the backyard, something about being alone together outside, with the brightly lit house behind them, made it seem as if they were on their own little island in the dark.

"I know what you mean," Bruce replied, almost in a whisper. "We're really looking at an old sky, the way the universe was billions of years ago. It's like a twinkling history book."

"Too bad Mr. Baker's history class isn't as interesting," she quipped.

She was drawn to him again, and she knew better. She could try to resist it, but she really didn't want to. Her feelings for him wouldn't go away by denying them. Yet something inside her made her break the mood.

"Speaking of school, have you asked Cheryl about the Senior Impersonation Night?" she asked, trying to sound as if she were just making casual conversation.

"Not yet. But I did ask her out. We're going to the movies tomorrow night."

Gayle felt as if all the air had been let out of her. Her worst fear had come true. But Bruce looked so wondrously happy, and, even though her own heart was breaking, she was too good a friend to spoil his mood.

"Are you worried? I mean, about tomorrow night?" she forced herself to continue.

"Well, it wasn't that bad asking her. In fact, it was a lot easier than I thought it would be. I waited for her by her locker after school today. When she saw me she got this big smile on her face. I—"

"That's okay, spare me the details. I know you'll have a good time," Gayle said. But Bruce was not so sure.

"I don't know. I'm a bit new at this. I mean, I don't have a lot of experience with girls," he said, stuffing his hands in his pockets.

Who does he think I am—Ann Landers? Gayle wondered. But she tried to reassure him. "Everybody is nervous on a first date. Cheryl will be as jumpy as you for the first few minutes, then it will all work out."

"Not her. She's been on a lot of dates. She'll be expecting..." He broke off, turning away from her slightly, obviously very embarrassed.

Gayle was surprised. Something was really bothering him. "You can tell me, Bruce. I know how you feel. I've been nervous on dates myself," she said, telling a small lie. She'd never had a date to be nervous on. *If only you knew,* she thought to herself, growing more

118

and more amused by her role.

"You're going to think I'm from the Stone Age, some sort of freak," he began, hesitantly.

"No, I won't. You can trust me," she coaxed him, her curiosity aroused.

"I feel so stupid," he began with a stammer and then blurted out, "I've never kissed a girl! I'm probably the only guy at Glenwood High who hasn't. Cheryl's going to expect one. I'm sure I'll do it wrong, and she'll notice, and I'll blow it. She'll think I'm a nerd or something."

There was a stunned silence. Gayle racked her brain, trying to think of how to reply. Good grief. Everything her friends had said about boys being blockheads was true—how could Bruce really be worried about something like that? Wouldn't nature just take its course?

This was certainly the old Bruce talking, not the Superhunk who'd invaded his body. "Oh, no, she won't," Gayle finally responded.

"Maybe if I...? Oh, I don't know," he stammered.

"What?" she asked, finding it increasingly difficult to keep a straight face.

"You girls have been teaching me to dance and flirt and everything. Maybe if I kissed you, you could tell me what I was doing wrong? I really could use your help."

Gayle's cheeks grew hot. She was so confused she didn't know whether to laugh or cry. *Her* teach *him*?

"I know it sounds dumb," Bruce continued, "but it's the only thing none of you taught me.

119

Please say you'll do it. Please kiss me, Gayle."

Those were the words she'd been dreaming he'd say. But it was wrong—all wrong! Gayle had fantasized this moment often, picturing them back up in the mountains, Bruce sheltering her from the cold with his warm, caring arms. He'd cradle her face in his palms and draw his lips close to hers, telling her over and over again, "I love you, Gayle..."

But that wasn't the way it was going to happen. Bruce only wanted to *use* her as a kissing surrogate. She, the expert, was supposed to teach him, the amateur. Furious at his assumption that she would play this scene, Gayle opened her mouth to tell him what she thought of his suggestion, when an idea struck her.

Why not turn it around so that *she* used *him*? Why not get some experience herself while she had the opportunity? Then after they'd finished kissing, she would let him have it. She'd tell Bruce he was the *worst* kisser she'd ever been with—she'd hurt him as badly as he'd hurt her.

"Okay, sure. I'd be happy to help you practice," Gayle said in a bold voice.

"Are you sure?" he asked tentatively.

"Oh yes, perfectly sure," she nodded, avoiding his eyes.

She raised her eyes to his and nodded again.

"Oh." He gulped and stalled a moment. He seemed uncertain where to start. Gayle smiled encouragingly. "First," she purred,

"You put your lips on mine..."

He looked at her, smiled nervously, then slowly stepped closer. Gently he put his hands on her shoulders and leaned toward her. She followed his soft eyes for as long as she could before she closed her own.

He lowered his face till his nose touched hers, then seemed uncertain which way to move to make his lips fit. Gayle snickered. Perhaps in reaction, Bruce's grip on her shoulders tightened. Tilting his head slightly, he pressed his lips on her mouth. Instinctively, Gayle felt her lips part as a flood of sensations overwhelmed her.

His kiss was gentle at first, but warm and reassuring. Despite herself, Gayle kissed back with genuine emotion, wrapping her arms around his back and holding on with all her might. She felt buoyed up and carried away, as if she were riding a wave into the black night. Soon there were no more thoughts of revenge, only of the sweetness of holding Bruce in her arms.

A moment later, Bruce paused, as if to draw back, and her heart skipped a beat. Then he drew her closer to him, with a kind of groan, and her skin tingled all over. She could feel his heart pounding. It was as if everything inside her was rushing to start a race, as if she had been struck by lightning from the storm rising up around them. And then she was lost again in their kiss.

They both broke away at the same time. Her

knees were so weak, she was afraid they might buckle. She was in love! That was all she knew; she couldn't think beyond that fact. But how did Bruce feel? She had no desire to hurt him now; in fact, she knew she never could have, anyway.

With his bright hazel eyes averted, his cheeks red with confusion, and his foot pawing the ground, Bruce appeared as affected as she was. But she wasn't sure. She wanted him to take her in her arms and kiss her again and tell her it was she, not Cheryl, that he loved.

"You're a great teacher," he finally said. He kept looking at the ground, avoiding her eyes. "You just saved my life."

Gayle felt as if she'd just been drenched with a bucket of water. Was that *all* he could say?

"Cheryl won't have any complaints. I'm sure," she said stiffly.

"Uh, thanks for coming over. It was a lot of fun looking at the stars with you," Bruce mumbled.

The surge of passion she had felt only moments before had been crushed by Bruce's apparent indifference. In its place, Gayle felt a fury she'd never before experienced surge up within her. With all her heart, she despised and loathed him.

"I hate you!" she shouted. Almost in a state of shock she slapped him across the face.

A look of hurt and confusion flashed across Bruce's flushed face. Then, just as suddenly, it was replaced by anger. "What do you mean?"

he cried, fury and frustration in his voice. "What did I do?"

Gayle turned and ran from him.

As she drove home, Gayle grew calmer; her emotions cleared, and a deep sense of hurt began to grow. She was crushed, humiliated, hurt, used, and misunderstood. Bruce acted as if he didn't even know she was a girl, someone with feelings just like Cheryl. He was selfish, concerned only with how to make a good impression on Cheryl. He didn't care if he broke her heart in the process.

At least she had one thing to be thankful for: no one knew about her inner feelings. It was going to be her secret. She wasn't even going to tell Lori about tonight. In fact, she was going to do what she should have done a long time ago. She was never going to think about Bruce again.

Chapter Eleven

Flips was crowded the following night, but just as vibrant and seductive as Gayle had remembered it. She stood for a moment searching the crowd, hoping she wouldn't recognize anyone. It was her night to be racy and wild, and she wanted to remain anonymous.

An hour earlier, Gayle had been content to spend that Friday night alone in her room, catching up on the homework due that Monday. But she couldn't concentrate. She had kept looking at the clock—and thinking about Bruce and Cheryl. At seven o'clock she had thought about Bruce standing before his bathroom mirror, splashing on that spicy-scented cologne she liked so much. At seven-thirty she'd pictured him driving up the long winding road that led to Cheryl's mansion overlooking Glenwood. At eight o'clock she'd imagined the two of them, arm-in-arm, walking into the Valley Cinema.

By eight-fifteen she'd had enough. She was making herself miserable, but for what? A boy who didn't know she was alive? Her psych teacher Mrs. Wiseman would call that aberrant behavior. Is that really how she wanted to live her life—hopelessly pining away over someone she could never have?

Gayle had slammed shut her history book with a resounding thud. The answer was no. She was no longer the fat nobody whom everybody made fun of. She was an attractive, outgoing, and desirable girl. Hadn't she found that out for herself when she'd gone to Flips?

That's when she got the idea to make a return trip to the disco. Only this time she'd dress more appropriately. After rummaging through the closet, she'd thrown together an outfit that Stephanie would say was "fit to kill." She'd begun with an old red skirt that fit her short, dumpy figure when she was twelve. It still fit her, only now the skirt was short and enticing. Over that she had put on a low-cut, black vest which buttoned down the front. She wore the vest without anything underneath. Patterned pantyhose, red flats, and dangling black earrings topped off the outfit wonderfully. Lori would have been proud of her, she'd thought, as she'd scampered out of her empty house.

A young woman interrupted her thoughts, asking if she wanted to check her coat. Slowly Gayle took it off and handed it over, not knowing what kind of reaction to expect. But she found out quickly.

Guys noticed her right away. Before she could even get settled Derek Johnson spotted her. He came over from across the dance floor. "Hi, Gayle. Boy, do you look great. Would you like to dance?" He asked as effortlessly as if he were an old friend.

"Thanks, Derek. I'd love to dance with a handsome guy like you," she said, looking him straight in the eye.

That was not where he had been looking, however, and his leering gaze sent a shiver of panic up her spine. When she had put on her black vest, she had thought it covered just enough. Now she felt half-naked. But the thought of Cheryl and Bruce having fun this very minute made something stiffen in Gayle's back. She could take care of herself. She was going to have fun, too!

She couldn't believe she had been so bold and he so confident. Derek probably expected girls to flirt with him, so while they danced Gayle really laid it on thick. She told him how sharp he looked in his tight jeans and aqua T-shirt—how his unstructured white jacket made him look like the sexy guy from *Miami Vice*. When other guys noticed her and smiled at her on the dance floor, Derek seemed to gloat as if she were his prized possession.

Gayle felt wonderful being the object of so much attention.

But when the DJ switched to a slow dance, she began to feel a little trapped by Derek's possessive attitude. He didn't even bother asking if she wanted to continue dancing. Moving in without any hesitation, he held her tightly and pressed against her. His warm, eager hands slid up and down her bare arms suggestively. He played with her hair and rubbed the back of her neck. Gayle felt as if she were dancing with Godzilla. He was all over her.

"I knew you were pretty, but I had no idea how gorgeous you were," he whispered in her ear, one hand seductively sliding down her lower back.

Gayle grimaced and held her breath. It was all happening too fast, and she began to sense she might be headed for trouble. She had to discourage Derek somehow.

As soon as the song came to a close, she made her move.

"Thank you, Derek. I think I'll rest a little. I'm a bit thirsty," she said, trying to untangle herself from his persistent grasp.

"I'll get you a drink," he offered, not to be discouraged.

"That's okay. I can get one myself."

"Oh, no. Have a seat. I'll be right back." And he was gone.

"Heaven help me," she said to no one in particular and resigned herself to a blue neon couch. But as soon as she sat down a new sense of panic swept through her like fire. Her skirt hitched up so far her panties almost showed! It was worse when she crossed her legs. There wasn't anything she could use to cover herself—Derek's wandering eyes would have a field day! How could she ever have thought she could wear this horrible thing! She fidgeted around madly, trying to find the least revealing posture. But it was hopeless.

When Derek returned with the soft drink, she was standing.

"Here," he began, handing her the glass. "Have a seat. Let's get comfortable."

"Actually, I'd rather stand. I can see more of the dancers," she said, grabbing the drink with both hands.

"Maybe we could go up to one of the higher couches in the back where it's quiet. You can see plenty from up there, but they can't see you."

"Maybe another time, Derek."

"Nah, c'mon. Let's move to the back, where it's secluded. I'd like to talk and get to know you better." The husky tone of his voice told her the "getting to know you" part had nothing to do with conversation. Gayle really felt in over her head now.

He gently put his arm around her shoulder and led her to one of the far corners of the disco.

One look at the dark, empty couches and Gayle knew she couldn't go through with it.

As he turned to sit down, he stopped and leaned in to give her a kiss. Frightened, she tried to pull away, but he lowered his arm to her waist and grasped her more tightly.

"No, Derek, no!" she pleaded.

"C'mon, Gayle, don't be a tease. I know you want it." Derek had both his arms around her now and was lowering her gently but firmly onto the back cushion of the couch.

"I said, stop it, Derek," Gayle said, her voice tense with fear. Without waiting for him to answer, she did the only thing she could to stop him. She took the drink still in her right hand and poured it over his head.

"What the—"Derek jumped back. The sticky liquid was dripping down his face and around the collar of his jacket. It was already leaving a blotchy stain in the center of his T-shirt.

"It was a mistake. I told you to leave me alone. I shouldn't have come here," Gayle burst out. She left him standing there, seemingly shocked speechless, as she ran to grab her coat and hurry out the crowded entrance.

The cool air of the night was a relief against her burning cheeks. She felt completely humiliated. Some revenge on Bruce! It had been as foolish and embarrassing a night as she could ever imagine. Even worse than the dance with Gaylord.

She climbed into her car and started to cry. What was wrong with her? Her head was spinning with all sorts of conflicting thoughts, and her whole body practically ached with the weight of her confused emotions. She needed to talk to someone who understood. Drying her eyes, she started the car and drove off.

"Gayle!" Lori cried out when she opened the door. "Am I glad to see you. I just started to make some brownies. You can make sure I only eat one."

Inside, the house was warm and filled with the delicious smell of baking brownies. It seemed so nice and comforting that Gayle's anxiety began to ease immediately.

"My mom's out for the evening and I didn't have anything to do. So you caught me red-handed, baking some temptation," Lori went on, as she scampered back into the kitchen.

Gayle took off her coat and, tossing it on the sofa, followed Lori through the living room back into the kitchen.

"What have you been doing tonight?" Lori asked. She was peering into the oven, checking the brownies' progress.

Gayle tried to answer, but suddenly she couldn't get her mouth to work. All her confused emotions welled up and stuck in her throat. So much had happened that Gayle didn't know where to start. She was on the verge of crying, when Lori turned around.

"They'll need at least fifteen more...Gayle! Where did you get an outfit like that!" Lori blurted out, finally noticing Gayle's short red skirt and skimpy black vest.

"Oh, Lori. It's terrible. I went dancing to-night and ..." She couldn't get the words out and started to cry.

"What happened, Gayle?" Lori asked, rushing to her side. She gave Gayle a comforting hug and let her cry on her shoulder.

"It's just that...I wanted it to..." Gayle kept stammering between sobs.

"Let's go in the living room and start from the beginning," Lori said, leading her friend out of the kitchen.

Once they got to the sofa the words began to pour out of Gayle's mouth like an open water faucet. Gayle told Lori about all the feelings she'd been hiding these past few weeks. How insecure she was about her new appearance, how she'd fallen in love with Bruce, and how she had decided to go to Flips so she could forget about his date with Cheryl. Gayle was amazed at how relieved she felt to finally talk out loud about the fears that had been bottled up so long. "So I decided to wear this outfit to prove I could be sexy, too, and get any boy I wanted," she concluded.

"Well, I'd say you succeeded. I'm not sure even Kit would ever wear anything quite like that," Lori commented.

"Yeah, some sexpot I turned out to be. Look what happens when I sit down!" Gayle giggled, with tears still falling.

"I noticed," chuckled Lori.

"Thank goodness I didn't sit down with

Derek!" Gayle said.

"Derek Johnson?" Lori sounded surprised, knowing all too well about his reputation.

"That's the worst part. He was the first guy who came up to me. I sort of wanted him to, at least I was really flattered he noticed me. But he was so aggressive. The way he looked at me I felt practically naked."

"I'm not surprised, knowing Derek. But you have to admit, Gayle, you *do* look practically naked."

"I know, but once it looked like Derek was going to kiss me, I got scared. It was terrible!" she gasped in remembrance of her embarrassment.

"Did he force himself on you?" Lori asked, getting really concerned.

"Well, he tried to sort of maneuver me onto the couch, and..."

"And?"

"I dumped Coke all over him and then started to cry," she moaned, chagrined.

"Good for you, it probably cooled him off. I wish I'd have thought of that on a few occasions," Lori said, starting to laugh.

"It's not funny!"

"But it is, Gayle," Lori insisted. "We all make mistakes when it comes to boys. The same kind of stuff has happened to me."

"I bet you didn't do anything as dumb as I did tonight," Gayle interrupted.

"A lot dumber. I almost lost Elaine's friendship over some birdbrain of a guy. And you know about Chris," Lori said softly.

"That was different," Gayle assured Lori.

"Yes, it was. But they were both still hard lessons to learn. You see, Gayle, what I mean is, tonight will be a funny memory some day, not a sad one. You'll get over it."

"But what about Monday morning when Derek tells the whole school what I did?" Gayle moaned.

"I don't think Derek's going to advertise this one," Lori said wisely.

Gayle shook her head ruefully. "I've sure turned into some kind of boy handler. First I slap Bruce in the face, then I douse Derek. What's happening to me?"

Lori cocked her head slightly and gave Gayle a look of exasperation she hadn't seen since she was fourteen and her mother caught her eating the Boston cream pie she'd bought for company. "Can't you see what's happening, Gayle? You're standing up for yourself now. When you first started losing weight, you were so desperate for attention you probably would have let Derek get away with anything he wanted. But tonight you were smart enough to realize you didn't have to take it—and you did something about it. I'm really proud of you."

"You are?" Gayle said, surprised. She started smiling. "But I made such a fool of myself."

"No one said it's easy, Gayle, and you have to admit you're making up for a lot of lost time. It's only natural you're going to make a bunch of mistakes. But you're learning."

"Yeah. I'm learning I'm not a fat nobody and I'm not a sex queen. So what am I?"

"Something in between?" Lori shrugged. "Believe me, I'm no expert, but I've learned the hard way myself that the best thing to be is yourself. When you're not sure what that is, just do what feels right."

"Funny you should say that, because that's exactly what I did with Bruce. When I first started getting to know him I didn't try to be somebody. I wasn't trying to impress him or prove anything. I was just being me. It was only after I started to fall in love with him that things really got mixed up."

"I think you've got to let Bruce be Bruce, too. I guess I hadn't really thought a lot about it until now, but he went through the exact thing. He had a lot of doubts about who he was, how he fit in around here. Operation Superhunk gave him the identity he felt he needed to be happy in Glenwood."

"Yeah, one that made him feel he had to get Cheryl," Gayle said, bitterly.

"That's not fair. He had a crush on Cheryl before we started in on him. I know he likes you as a friend, Gayle, if that makes a difference."

"I know that, too, Lori. But it's not enough for me. Not anymore."

"Well, if he refuses to see what a wonderful person you are, then all I can say is that it's his loss. I know there are plenty of other guys who'd be interested in you."

Gayle remembered the way Mark looked at her the day she helped him with the poster. Maybe if she kept her eyes open she'd discover more Marks—or more importantly— someone really special who could make her forget about Bruce. 'Yeah. I guess you're right. It's not like I didn't know Bruce had a crush on Cheryl all along. I guess that's the way it goes," she said thoughtfully.

"Oh, no! The brownies! I better check them," exclaimed Lori and she jumped up and ran to the kitchen.

"You know, Lori, you're pretty special. It's not everybody who has a friend who will listen to silly problems and still share her brownies with them," Gayle said, smiling gratefully as she helped Lori remove the hot brownies from the tray.

"No problem. Just as long as you let me eat only one!" Lori pleaded.

"And vice versa?" countered Gayle.

"It's a deal!"

They both dug in. Then Lori began to giggle.

"What's so funny?"

"I can't stop thinking about Derek. He must have looked awful!"

"Like a wet mop," Gayle said, starting to giggle herself. Lori was right, she realized: things didn't seem half as bad anymore when she was able to laugh at them.

Chapter Twelve

Gayle was finishing the last little bit of her yogurt the following morning when a car pulled into the driveway. She'd never been so galvanized by a plain blue Pontiac before. It was Bruce! What could he possibly want?

Whatever it was, she couldn't let him see her dressed like this! She dashed up to her room and quickly pulled on a green sweater over her pin-striped demins. She clipped her red hair back with high crowned marbled combs. As she came down the stairs her mind was racing. Why was he here? If he thought she'd want to hear about his date last night, he could think again! She was going to play it cool.

As she came down the stairs her mother was running up, to let her know a "friend" was waiting for her. Gayle saw a mixture of hope and happiness on her face. Maybe her mother *did* love her and want the best for her, Gayle thought. Gayle hated the idea of telling her mother it was a false alarm, that Bruce wasn't interested in her. She would be terribly disappointed.

Bruce was sitting on the white leather couch in the living room. Gayle had to steel herself not to react to how great he looked, dressed in a simple pair of jeans and a striped polo shirt.

"Hello, Bruce," she said, coolly. Her insides, however, were in a knot of anticipation.

He didn't answer at first. He seemed a bit anxious and unsure of himself. He glanced at the white carpet and nervously scratched an imaginary line with the toe of his Reeboks. "I'm sorry, Gayle—" His voice was barely a whisper.

Gayle wasn't sure she heard right. "What?" she asked. She took a seat on the matching sofa across the glass coffee table from him.

"—For being such a nerd," he said, looking up.

"You, a nerd? Bruce Fletcher, Mr. Super-hunk? The master of seduction? The captain of cool? Don't tell me all the lessons we girls have given you haven't stuck?" Gayle's voice was dripping with sarcasm.

"I know you hate me, Gayle, and right now I think you've got every right to feel that way. I've really made a big mess of everything, and if you want me to leave I will. But before I go, I'd like to say what's on my mind." He looked at her expectantly, his hazel eyes clouded with an emotion Gayle couldn't decipher.

"I suppose. Go on and get it over with," she said.

"It really floored me when you slapped me the other night," he began. "I stood there for a long time, wondering what in blazes I'd done to deserve it. Finally I went inside—only to be greeted by my mother, who asked me where you went. I just blurted out to her what happened. And do you know what she said to me?" He didn't wait for Gayle to answer. "She said, 'Bruce, can't you see that girl likes you?'" He paused. "Is it true, Gayle? Is she right?"

Gayle continued to glare at him, afraid to speak, even to move. She didn't know how to deal with the mountain of emotions building inside her.

Bruce nodded. "That's okay, you don't have to answer now. After Mom said that I felt like banging my head against the wall. Everything began to make sense to me. The car, the storm, the photos, the dance, the kiss. I understand . . . can you forgive me for being so dumb?"

Maybe it made sense to Bruce, but now Gayle was more confused than ever. "Dumb about what?"

"For not realizing I've liked you all along," Bruce explained. "Superhunk's been super thickheaded. But now I know I care for you. In fact, I have ever since the day of the egg toss."

"You have?" Gayle couldn't believe what she was hearing. It had to be a dream.

But it wasn't. "I didn't stop to analyze it, Gayle. All I knew was that I liked being with you. I didn't have to pretend to be anybody special; you seemed to accept me, faults and all. You were always interested in what I had to say—like, you're the only girl I've met in Glenwood who's even heard of the Cubs. I started looking forward to seeing you, even making excuses so I could."

"Like when you helped me frame the photos?"

"Yeah, and when I came over to look at your camera."

"I thought you were just curious about photography."

"No, it was more. I didn't understand it myself, though, until the day of that storm. When we were up on that mountain something came over me, and I wanted to kiss you. But then you pulled away, and I was afraid to try again."

"But you should have!" Gayle cried, unable to control herself any more. "I wanted to kiss you, too, but I was so afraid to tell you. I thought you thought it had been a mistake. But it's true, I *do* like you."

"Why didn't you tell me?" he asked.

"Why didn't *you* tell *me*?" she countered.

"I didn't know what to say. I was afraid you'd

laugh at me."

"So was I!" Gayle exclaimed, shaking her head in disbelief. "I didn't know what to do. Bruce, I've never felt this way about a boy before."

"You haven't? Surely, one of your other boy-friends—"

Gayle dismissed this with a wave of her hand. "The truth is, I have as little experience with boys as you do with girls. I don't know how you got it in your head that I did."

"Come on, Gayle, someone as pretty as you—"

"I used to look different." Gayle got up and walked to the white baby grand piano in the corner of the room. Without a moment's hesitation she picked up one of the family photos on it and brought it over to Bruce. "See that?" she pointed to the hefty girl seated between two smiling parents. "That was me a year ago. Pretty piggy, huh?" Gayle searched his face for revulsion but to her relief and joy she found none.

Bruce shrugged. "Looks like you with more weight on your bones," was all he said.

Gayle couldn't believe it. All this time, she'd been so afraid of what Bruce would think if he'd known how fat she'd been. And he didn't even care! She was so happy she felt like kissing him. So that's exactly what she did. Right there in the middle of her parents' living room she leaned over and kissed him.

To her delight he returned the kiss passionately. A thrill ran up her spine, and she felt waves of warmth radiate from inside. This time it wasn't just practice. It was love.

"It'll take more than a bolt of lightning to scare me off now." He smiled, holding her in his arms.

But there was still one unanswered question. "What about Cheryl?"

Bruce looked at her sheepishly. "I'm sorry. I really rubbed her in your face, didn't I? Anyway, I won't be seeing her anymore."

"So she dumped you last night, huh?"

Bruce grinned. "More like the other way around. I can't believe I was stupid enough to fall for her. That girl did nothing but talk about herself—through the entire movie, no less. I couldn't wait to take her home. The whole time I was with her all I could think about was how much more fun it would have been if I were with you."

"You don't know how great it is to hear that."

"Good. 'Cause that makes my next question a little easier. I know I'm late, but would you be my Ginger Rogers?" He flashed a smile, but still looked very uncertain.

Gayle was ecstatic, so stunned with happiness that all she could do was throw her arms around him again. Bruce picked her up and spun her around the living room joyfully. After they drew apart, she whispered, "Does that answer it for you?"

For several minutes they sat on the sofa,

Gayle nestled comfortably in the crook of Bruce's arm, as they adjusted to the change in their relationship. Then Bruce began seriously, "There's another thing. I've been thinking lately that I'm not really comfortable with the superhunk image you and your friends worked up for me. Don't get me wrong, I really needed the driving lessons and the dancing lessons and a revamp of my wardrobe—but no matter how hard Alex tries I'm never going to like surfing and I'll never be Stephanie's idea of cool. It's just not me."

"What about the sunglasses?" she wondered.

"In the garbage," he said, snorting.

"Then that's just fine by me. I was kind of fond of the old Bruce, anyway—even with egg on his face," she kidded him.

"I should've known—considering you're the one who threw it."

"Do you want to start practicing now?" she asked. "We can. My dad's out golfing as usual, and Mom's about to go out grocery shopping."

"We've got time. Right now, there's something more important," he said.

"What?"

"The street fair. We have to go see your photos."

The street fair was already crowded by the time they got there. Glenwood Drive had been cordoned off, with booths arranged on both sides. The place was filled with townspeople and weekend visitors browsing around, looking at the incredible selection of crafts, including pottery, leather goods, stained glass, strange mobiles, raw honey, ethnic foods, and beautiful handmade quilts. A troupe of clowns roaming the area entertaining the crowds helped contribute to the festive atmosphere.

"I wonder where the photography competition is?" asked Bruce.

"We'll find it. Let's just browse around and look at the things they've got," she said, genuinely interested in the crafts. She also appreciated the crowded conditions that forced them to stay close together, arms intertwined.

As they walked, she spotted Alex and Wes crossing the street to the Belgian waffle booth. Gayle was about to call out to them, when she noticed they seemed to have eyes only for each other. Gayle finally knew what that feeling was like, and she didn't want to interrupt them. Besides, being with Bruce in this special way was such a heady new sensation that she wanted to savor it as long as she could.

It was then she noticed Stephanie trailing behind Alex and Wes. Gayle could tell that Stephanie felt like a third wheel, and that was something she understood well enough to write a book about.

"Hey, Stephanie!" she called out, waving at her to join them.

Stephanie waved back, then hurried to catch up with them.

"Come on with us. We're going to see how I did in the photo competition," Gayle said as Stephanie arrived.

"Oh, really?" Stephanie replied rather strangely.

She and Bruce exchanged furtive glances.

"I can use the moral support," Gayle added, deciding to ignore the exchange, at least for the moment.

"Looks like you're doing okay," whispered Stephanie, motioning to Bruce, who had moved slightly ahead of them to a snack stand.

Gayle gave her an "I'll tell you later" look. Munching on popcorn, they continued up the last block.

"Here it is!" Bruce called out.

They had arrived at the competition section. There were areas for paintings and drawings, leather goods, pottery, sculpture, fabrics, and, of course, the one for photography.

"Gayle, come here — quick!" shouted Bruce.

Gayle hurried over to his side. On a pegboard panel was her photograph of the lightning bolt — with a blue ribbon next to it. She couldn't believe her eyes. She'd won!

"Way to go, Gayle," Stephanie called out.

Bruce didn't hesitate a moment, giving her a kiss of congratulation right in front of Stephanie. Stephanie's chin dropped a foot in surprise, but she didn't say a thing. She looked very pleased for them both. Gayle herself was beaming, although most of the joy was not because of the blue ribbon. She'd take a kiss like that over a blue ribbon any day.

"I couldn't have done it without your help, Bruce," she said gratefully.

"What did you do?" asked Stephanie, a little confused.

"I held the umbrella." He laughed.

"He's being modest, as usual," Gayle interjected. "Bruce helped frame it, and I would never have entered it without his encouragement. Everyone's encouragement," she said, truly thankful for all her friends' support.

"Maybe I can be your assistant when you're famous," Bruce went on, ignoring her remark. "I can hold an umbrella for you in the rain, a parasol in the sun, fan you when it's too warm, cuddle you when the temperature drops..."

"Oh, Bruce, quit kidding." Gayle laughed.

"Don't knock it. Sounds pretty good to me," Stephanie said, with more than a little trace of envy in her voice.

"Hey, congratulations Gayle!" shouted Alex, who had just arrived with Wes. While they were praising Gayle's work, Lori, Elaine, Carl, Kit, Justin, and Ginger showed up, too.

"Surprise!" they all shouted.

"Where did you guys come from?" gasped Gayle.

"Bruce told us," Lori answered.

"We wanted to share in the good news," said Kit.

"I came by early and saw the blue ribbon. So I called Kit, and she helped arrange everything," he explained.

"You knew! You clown," Gayle exclaimed.

"Wait a minute, didn't you enter three pictures?" Lori asked.

"Yeah, I wonder where they are?"

"Over here. Remember the one with the shells?" called out Elaine. They all hurried over to see Gayle's other photos, which hung together on a different panel. Neither had a ribbon.

"Too bad, but one blue ribbon is nothing to complain about," offered Elaine.

"That's okay, I'm amazed the judges liked any of them," Gayle said, not at all disappointed.

"I don't know how they could have chosen among them. In fact, I like this one better," Carl spoke up, as he pointed to the picture of the doll on the beach.

"The rules state only one award to a photographer," Bruce explained. "I already asked about that. I thought they all should have gotten ribbons."

"Yeah, I think Bruce is right. They all deserved a blue ribbon," Lori said, smiling a secret smile that told Gayle how happy she was about the way things had turned out.

Gayle had never dreamed things would work out so well. Her photographs were a suc-

147

cess. The "look" was in Bruce's eyes when he gazed at her. Best of all, her friends were there to help her enjoy it all.

Chapter Thirteen

Gayle peeked through the backstage curtains of the school auditorium at the full house. She and Bruce were on next. She made a final check of her costume: A strapless velvet halter top with a full circle skirt in the perfect shade of peach to go with her hair, dyed to match peau de soie pumps, seamed hosed, and the absolutely stunning touch from her mother's cedar chest in the attic—a white fur stole. It was only rabbit, but it looked elegant, and they had managed to work it into their routine. She looked at Bruce in his top hat and tails and smiled in anticipation. They had to wait only for the cue.

The two weeks she'd had to prepare for the Senior Impersonation Night had been so marvelously romantic and exciting that Gayle worried if the evening itself could ever live up to her expectations. Not a day had gone by that she and Bruce hadn't been together. As they had practiced their routine, the romantic mood of the old movies and songs they hoped to recreate had swept them into their own little enchantment. In the past Gayle might have been afraid that the show would mark the end of the magic, but inside she knew this time she wouldn't turn into a pumpkin.

Thanks to Kit's choreography they had a routine Gayle felt was something special. But she didn't know if her stomach would survive the anticipation.

She and Bruce had a hard act to follow. Earlier in the show Kit had performed, dressed in her Shirley Temple ringlet wig and a baby doll dress. She had begun with a little tap dance number and a lullaby song. But halfway into the song she threw off her wig and tore off her dress, finishing with a high-kicking, shoe-stomping, hard-dancing number in nothing but a skin-tight red leotard. She'd practically brought down the house.

It seemed to take forever for the MC to announce them, but as soon as the opening strains of Cole Porter's "Why Shouldn't I" came over the loudspeakers they were on!

Bruce took her hand and led her onstage. Dramatically she let the fur stole slide off her shoulders and drag across the stage before she tossed it to one side.

Gayle didn't remember a thing after that. It

was like a dream she could feel, but not recall. Later everyone told her how graceful they had been and how they made the perfect couple. Other girls asked Gayle to teach them how to dance, and everyone said they were almost as good as the real Ginger Rogers and Fred Astaire. But in Gayle's mind, their act was one big glorious glowing sensation. And then it was over.

Bruce guided her off the stage, and the applause broke through her mind. He was grinning from ear to ear.

"You were great!" he said, hugging her.

"So were you." She laughed.

That was when the real fun began. Everyone there went to the party dance in the gymnasium dressed as their favorite celebrity, and Bruce and Gayle were two of the first arrivals. The dance floor was fairly empty, and they both had their eye on it. But before they could head for the open floor, Stephanie and Lori came up to congratulate them on their routine.

Stephanie had actually come as Marilyn Monroe, just as Gayle herself had jokingly said she wanted to do. Stephanie looked the part in her wig and padded bra. Lori was dressed as Greta Garbo in a florid dress right out of *Camille*. She looked stunning.

"You look great as a blonde, Stephanie," said Gayle.

"Perhaps, but I refuse to admit that blondes have more fun," she kidded.

"Stick around and find out," flirted Bruce.

"I will if you promise me a dance, big boy," Stephanie purred.

"That sounds more like Mae West," said Gayle.

"Blondes. You see one, you've seen 'em all," Stephanie joked as she sashayed away with Bruce in tow.

"Speaking of hair, look at Elaine!" gasped Lori.

Elaine and Carl had just walked in together, and Gayle had never seen a more unlikely-looking couple. Elaine was dressed as Cindy Lauper, Carl as a bearded man with glasses and a cane.

"Elaine, how did you do that to your hair!" gasped Alex.

"Kit promised it would wash out. I'll kill her if it doesn't," Elaine answered.

"If you don't mind me asking, who are you, Carl?" Gayle asked.

"Mmmm, I find it quite significant that you should ask me that question," Carl hinted, his response appropriately dignified and aloof.

"Sigmund Freud?" blurted out Lori.

"Precisely." He smiled.

"I didn't know he was an entertainer," countered Gayle, with a baiting smile.

"One of the greatest, my dear, one of the greatest," Carl murmured in his most officious voice.

Stephanie and Bruce rejoined the group after their brief turn on the floor. Everyone was still checking out the costumes.

"Oh, my gosh. Look at Ginger!" interrupted Elaine.

Ginger and Craig were handling the refreshments, which featured Ginger's Gingery Cookies and punch. Craig was dressed as a butler, but Ginger towered over everyone in her Gumby costume.

"She gets my prize as best costume. But, Elaine, you're a close second," said Bruce.

"Well, as a consolation I think the least you can do is dance with me, Bruce," Elaine said.

"You bet. I *love* Cyndi Lauper," Bruce agreed as he led her toward the floor.

Gayle tried not to feel disappointed that Bruce had yet to dance with her. She remembered too well the night at the disco. Would Bruce get carried away again and not notice her?

Then she grinned, realizing how she'd almost allowed herself to slip into her old pattern of self-doubt. All Bruce was doing was dancing with a friend!

I've got better things to do with my energy than worry! she chided herself.

As soon as Bruce and Elaine finished dancing, she hurried over to him.

He smiled at her as if it had been hours — not minutes — since he'd seen her. "Now here's the partner I've been waiting for," he said.

"How about a few turns on the floor to make the girls jealous and then some quiet moments in the corner?" she said.

"It's a deal."

As they worked their way to the middle of the dance floor, Gayle saw Stephanie dancing with Rick Forrester, who was clad in a Little Abner costume. It was a slow song and they were very close. It looked as if they saw only each other, and Gayle hoped it was the beginning of something special for her friend. True, their backgrounds were different, but anything could happen where love was involved. She and Bruce were the perfect example.

Gayle smiled, put her head on Bruce's shoulder as he took her in his arms, and reminded herself that love could be found in the strangest of places—even in the middle of a thunderstorm.

A LOVE TRILOGY
First there is <u>LOVING</u>.

Meet Caitlin, gorgeous, rich, charming and wild And anything Caitlin wants she's used to getting So when she decides that she wants handsome Jed Michaels, there's bound to be some trouble.

Then there is <u>LOVE LOST</u>.

The end of term has arrived and it looks like the summer will be a paradise But tragedy strikes and Caitlin's world turns upside down Will Caitlin speak up and risk sacrificing the most important thing in her life?

And at last, <u>TRUE LOVE</u>.

Things are just not going the way Caitlin had planned, and she can't seem to change them! Will it take a disaster and a near-fatality for people to see the light?

SENIORS

We hope you enjoyed reading this book. All the titles currently available in the Seniors series are listed at the front of the book. They are all available at your local bookshop or newsagent, though should you find any difficulty in obtaining the books you would like, you can order direct from the publisher, at the address below. Also, if you would like to know more about the series, or would simply like to tell us what you think of the series, write to:

Kim Prior
Seniors
Transworld Publishers Ltd.
61–63 Uxbridge Road
Ealing
London W5 5SA

To order books, please list the title(s) you would like, and send together with a cheque or postal order made payable to TRANSWORLD PUBLISHERS LTD. Please allow the cost of the book(s) plus postage and packing charges as follows:

All orders up to a total of £5.00: 50p
All orders in excess of £5.00: Free

Please note that payment must be made in pounds sterling; other currencies are unacceptable.

(The above applies to readers in the UK and Republic of Ireland only)

If you live in Australia or New Zealand and would like more information about the series, please write to:

Sally Porter
Seniors
Transworld Publishers (Aust) Pty Ltd.
15-23 Helles Avenue
Moorebank
N.S.W. 2170
AUSTRALIA

Kiri Martin
Seniors
c/o Corgi and Bantam Books
New Zealand
Cnr. Moselle and Waipareira Avenues
Henderson
Auckland
NEW ZEALAND